DID YOU EVER HEAR A RAISIN TALKING?

Linda should have been prepared after hearing the other kids laughing, but somehow, when she turned the corner, the last thing she expected to bump into was a large object that resembled an overgrown raisin. Candy's first costume had struck Linda as funny only because she thought it was just one of Candy's stunts that wouldn't last. Now it was obvious she was wrong. Candy was out to prove something.

"Everyone thinks you're nuts," Linda whispered, hoping not too many people noticed the conversation.

"Well, I think everyone in this school is nuts." Candy pointed to a vulgar crayoned message scribbled on the wall. "You'll never catch a raisin doing *that* . . ."

If You Can't Be The Sun, Be A Star

Bestsellers from SIGNET VISTA

(0451)

☐ **TWO POINT ZERO** by Anne Snyder and Louis Pelletier.
(114760—$1.75)*

☐ **TWO BLOCKS DOWN** by Jina Delton. (114779—$1.50)*

☐ **THE CLIFFS OF CAIRO** by Elsa Marston. (115309—$1.75)*

☐ **TWO LOVES FOR JENNY** by Sandy Miller. (115317—$1.75)*

☐ **OVER THE HILL AT FOURTEEN** by Jamie Callan.
(115740—$1.75)*

☐ **PLEASE DON'T KISS ME NOW** by Merrill Joan Gerber.
(115759—$1.95)*

☐ **ANDREA** by Jo Stewart. (116542—$1.75)*

☐ **ANNE AND JAY** by Barbara Bartholomew. (116550—$1.75)*

☐ **IF YOU CAN'T BE THE SUN, BE A STAR** by Harriet May Savitz. (117557—$2.25)*

☐ **NOBODY'S BROTHER** by Anne Synder and Louis Pelletier.
(117565—$2.25)*

☐ **ALICE WITH GOLDEN HAIR** by Eleanor Hull.(117956—$1.95)*

☐ **A SHADOW LIKE A LEOPARD** by Myron Levoy.
(117964—$2.25)*

*Prices slightly higher in Canada

If You Can't Be The Sun, Be A Star

HARRIET MAY SAVITZ

A SIGNET VISTA BOOK

NEW AMERICAN LIBRARY

TIMES MIRROR

Publisher's Note

This novel is a work of fiction. Names, characters, places, and incidents are either the product of the author's imagination or are used fictitiously, and any resemblance to actual persons, living or dead, events, or locales is entirely coincidental.

Copyright © 1982 by Harriet May Savitz

RL 6/IL 6+

SIGNET VISTA TRADEMARK REG. U.S. PAT. OFF. AND FOREIGN COUNTRIES REGISTERED TRADEMARK—MARCA REGISTRADA HECHO EN CHICAGO, IL., U.S.A.

SIGNET, SIGNET CLASSICS, MENTOR, PLUME, MERIDIAN AND NAL BOOKS are published by The New American Library, Inc., 1633 Broadway, New York, New York 10019

First Printing, August, 1982

1 2 3 4 5 6 7 8 9

PRINTED IN THE UNITED STATES OF AMERICA

Acknowledgments

My gratitude to Dr. Joseph DiMino, for sharing his belief in people. . . . My thanks to Chief of Police John A. Volpe and the Plymouth Township Police Department for their guidance. . . . My special appreciation for the use of the poem, *Be The Best of Whatever You Are*, by Douglas Malloch. . . . My love to Ira, Sue, Amy, and David Blatstein.

1

It was a gray day, with the sky clouded over. Through the school window Candy watched the thin limbs of the trees stir in the winter wind. The Christmas holiday was over, a vacation spent mainly with friends commuting to a nearby ski slope.

The gifts had been exchanged, the parties attended. Now the holiday was just another pleasant memory and the stark reality of January was at hand. A new year had begun . . . another year without her father.

It would be three years on January 12 that he last left the house to go to the Township Building, where he would sit behind the desk marked POLICE SERGEANT and tend to the business of the police department. But on that day he had stopped briefly to look in on a friend, and that small detour altered not only her own life but that of her mother and of her brother, Ian.

At nine o'clock in the morning, Pop Williams' store had been closed. It was always open at eight-thirty, rain or shine. Pop's fruit and vegetables could be found in cartons on the sidewalk, waiting for eager customers to pick through them. But that day the shades were drawn, the door shut, the sidewalk empty. Sergeant Miller, worried about his old friend, had stopped his patrol car, "just to take a look," he told the policeman in whose arms he died.

Inside the store he had found Pop dead. The bullets that then tore into his own back came from behind the stacked cartons of vegetables. The murderer, apparently surprised in the middle of a robbery, escaped without leaving a clue. The vegetable store was now a bowling alley and three years had passed.

Candy's attention remained on the stark portrait outside. She was reminded of winter's weakness, its lack of color, except for an occasional snowstorm glistening white, or now and then a red cardinal perched atop one of the barren branches. The persistent wind crept between the cracks of the old windows in the classroom. Candy drew her sweater about her shoulders. The school, in its attempt to conserve energy, kept the thermostat at sixty-five degrees. Everyone was encouraged to wear heavy clothes. No one stated what those clothes had to look like. Candy pulled up the thick leotards which always managed to sag down about her thin legs.

The teacher, Mrs. Murphy, stood in front of her desk, her book, as was Candy's, opened to a page of facts on crime. Candy tapped her pencil gently against her notebook, suddenly realizing she had never seen Mrs. Murphy in a skirt or a dress. Not once since the beginning of the year. Usually she wore slacks of a better quality than most ever seen around Stanley High, but never high heels or fancy stockings.

"Let's get into the causes of wolf packs," Mrs. Murphy persisted.

Candy didn't feel like thinking about the groups of young gangs who robbed shoppers in the downtown section, and who were now moving slowly up the avenue, threatening even her own neighborhood. These bands of thieves were known to openly prowl the streets looking for a robbery victim. Memories of Pop Williams came flooding back.

"I dread your going downtown alone," Candy's mother would caution, as if she were entering a war zone. Neither wanted to admit that in the not too distant future they could be feeling the same way about just stepping from their front door.

It had become downright dangerous on certain downtown streets, though there were some friends who dared go there, bringing back tales of necklaces being ripped from necks, pocketbooks yanked off arms. In broad daylight. In the very center of traffic. Groups of young people, mostly Candy's age, approached anyone they chose, circling their victim, then fleeing into the crowds with whatever they managed to steal.

Mrs. Murphy discussed their impact on society. The class took notes. "Fear and the inability to fight back are the wolf pack's allies."

Police Sergeant Miller had gone past the fear but never had the chance to fight back. He was shot from behind. Five hundred fellow policemen attended his funeral. The funeral home was packed with flowers.

"Crime in our city is now out of control," Mrs. Murphy calmly continued, as if she were giving a weather forecast.

It depressed Candy and even angered her that the once most fashionable part of town was now as forbidden as the forests she used to read about in fairy tales. Only, the wicked witch had been replaced by the wolf pack. There was no magic wand available to wipe it away.

From her humanities class, Candy went on to ecology, where the teacher, Mr. Parker, stressed the danger of pollution in water and air. She listened with little enthusiasm as Mr. Parker cautioned, "If we keep on at this rate of destruction, soon the air we breathe, the water we drink, will poison us." Mr. Parker wore a large dotted shirt which accented his wide frame. He was famous for his own private dress code. At no time did his shirt and trousers appear to be comfortable on his massive body. The shirt was usually sticking out from one end or the other. A button was almost always certain to be missing. He never wore a tie. His hair, thick and black, hung long to his shoulders.

Before the last parent-teacher meeting, he warned his students, "Better prepare your parents for this," he said, pointing to the hair and loud orange shirt, "so they'll not be shocked by what they see." He laughed as he said it, but underneath the humor was a serious request that parents be cautioned on his choice of outlandish clothes.

Candy tried to picture him with short hair and a white shirt. She thought he might have attained a gentle handsomeness. She shifted in her seat, already tiring of the game she often found herself playing lately. The game of make-believe consisted of selecting someone dressed sloppily, perhaps with overalls, long hair, thick lipstick, whatever the case happened to be, then mentally changing their clothes and creating a new image for them. It was almost like being a designer.

She sometimes even imagined her classmates smiling. Looking about the classroom, she realized that at that moment there was not even one moderately friendly expression. Everyone stared ahead as if they were machines operating in a large factory with one thing in common: they were all smileless. Even Mr. Parker. Of course, lately there wasn't much to feel good about. In between classes it was as if a blanket of tension had fallen over the entire school, suffocating any possible good times. A small group now seemed to fill the halls with subtle fear and spread their mood throughout the majority of Candy's classmates.

Candy tried to recall when things began to change, and after some serious thought she realized the school had undergone a severe transformation when the dress code, along with many other restrictions, had been suddenly dropped. It was certainly taken away without anyone asking Candy for *her* consent. If they had inquired, she would have strongly argued for a more explicit dress guide.

Those who had pushed the guidelines out had done so as if there could be no opposition. There wasn't.

Little by little, the clothes around her had altered from relaxed to sloppy. The people inside the clothes changed also. It was as if everyone around her had broken free to be themselves, only now they weren't quite sure what that self was.

"Did you ever notice it?" she mentioned to her friend Linda while walking to the lunchroom early that afternoon. "Nobody laughs around here anymore. It's just all become one big gripe."

"Look, I've got my own problems." Linda sat down at the lunch table and took a bite of her sandwich. "My nose didn't really turn out the way I thought it would." A long sigh accompanied the statement.

Candy studied the remodeled feature on Linda's face. The long-awaited nose job, the one that had finally taken place over the Christmas holidays, had settled now into its new shape. However, it still didn't look as though it quite belonged to Linda.

"It looks fine to me," Candy said with a degree of honesty. "There's no bump on it anymore." It looked better than her own, she thought. Candy's mother assured her that her Grecian nose, accompanied by dark hair and eyes, gave her a "strong, purposeful look, not just another common face."

"Oh, I know the bump's gone," Linda agreed, "but I think it tilts up too much. Even Pete noticed it."

Candy shook her head, staring down into her carton of milk. She knew better than to get into a discussion concerning Linda's new boyfriend, Pete, who always seemed to have trouble riding close behind him.

She was also tired of talking about Linda's nose. Ever since she had become her friend back in grammar school, when Linda and her family had moved next door, it was the nose that monopolized their conversation. Each day, going to and coming from school, at some point, it would creep into the discussion.

"It's a horrible bump and I hate it," Linda would repeat over and over.

Then, as they grew older, Linda persisted until at last her parents agreed. On her sixteenth birthday . . . the birthday gift . . . a new nose. They had all looked forward to it, Linda, her parents, and Candy, perhaps most of all, for she feared if she had to discuss the bump very much longer, it might seriously damage their friendship.

Now she realized it wasn't over yet. Instead of the bump, there was the tilt. Candy had believed the operation would end it. She wondered if anything could. Maybe Linda would never be satisfied.

"I picked up the newspaper this morning," Candy said, biting into her tuna-fish sandwich and pausing, trying for a change in subject, hoping to avoid a return to the nose operation, or Pete. The first depressed her. The second only angered her and put a further strain on the already shaky relationship between Linda and herself. There seemed to be more topics to avoid lately than to share. "On the front page was an article on some girl our age dying of

7

leukemia. She had a scarf on her head because she was bald from the treatments. The entire article went into detail about her feelings and the reaction of her parents. All about her suffering, and what she thought about dying. You know, I hate to even read the newspapers lately. The news is all so down!"

"If I'm really uncomfortable with the nose, the doctor said he could adjust it," Linda said, as though she hadn't heard a word.

Candy was tempted to adjust it immediately, free of charge, with an accidental jab of her left elbow or even a misguided fist. But she knew she could never hurt her friend that way. She owed Linda for the long months after her father's death, when Linda had stuck by her through the tears that kept coming each time someone offered condolence. How many times it had been said, "We're sorry about your father." Being sorry didn't bring him back. Catching his killer might have brought some relief from the pain.

Candy continued her one-way conversation. "You know, I wanted to tell all those people around that girl, the doctors and the reporters, to just let her have her privacy. Maybe she wouldn't die on the date they forecast. I wouldn't. Just for spite, I'd stay alive." She bit into a cookie. "Doesn't a story like that bother you?"

Now it was Linda's turn to look annoyed. Her green eyes narrowed as if she were looking at an enemy rather than a friend. "You don't even know the girl. What are you worrying about her for?" The implication was that Candy should be worrying about Linda's problem instead.

If indeed Candy was to worry about Linda, it would not be about her already attractive physical appearance but rather about her friend of questionable character, Pete Fields.

"Don't you understand? She has nothing to smile about. She could be you or me."

Linda wrinkled her new nose and unwrapped her cupcake. One finger absentmindedly went up and down the sleek creation above her mouth. "I always feel it happens to someone else."

"You're lucky." Candy crunched on an apple. "I feel it could happen to me, and if I don't help change things, it might." She was not thinking of the girl with leukemia now. She was thinking of the wolf packs, the unsafe city streets, and of her school and the faces growing more lifeless each day.

Linda shrugged away the problem. "Candy, you're the happiest person I know." Her sarcasm did not go unnoticed.

Usually Candy accepted her friend's sharp wit easily, but today it felt like a slap against her skin. She threw her lunch bag in the trash can. "The thing is," Candy persisted after a moment's silence, trying to recapture Linda's interest, "no one seems to care what they do to anyone else anymore."

"There's Pete!" Linda exclaimed, her strawberry hair flying as she ran in his direction, deserting Candy in midstream. "See you later," she called.

From lunch on, the day twisted, filled with nothing but crevices and wrong turns. A test came back unfinished. A homework assignment was forgotten in her bedroom in her pocketbook, which she had also left behind. A boy who had thrown a trash can at the teacher the day before, was returned to class. Candy resented it. Just as she resented her father's killer never being caught.

But it was at the end of the day that she was dealt the final blow. Someone had broken the lock on her locker. She knew even before she opened the door, as one sometimes senses bad news before it is delivered, her new ski jacket would be missing. It was. Linda loaned her a heavy sweater she kept in her locker. They walked home in silence.

Another jacket would have to be purchased. Money was tight. Her mother, who held a full-time job as a secretary, kept reminding her of that. She would not receive the news well.

There was no hiding the fact her jacket had been stolen. The moment Candy walked into the house, her mother stared at the bulky sweater, too short in the sleeves.

"They didn't," she yelled, drying her hands and running to the telephone all at once. She left her mother in the kitchen, the words, "I would like to meet with the principal," drifting behind Candy up the hall steps toward her bedroom. She could have predicted what her mother's reaction would be. First a call to the principal, then to the superintendent of schools, and then, if all else failed, to the school board.

Her two pets lay on the bed sharing a spot of sun. Her beagle cozily tucked around Tiger, the cat.

Candy wondered at the ease of their coexistence and wished it could be as easy elsewhere. There was still a small spot of sun not occupied beside them. She slid onto the bed, resting her head on her arm. The sun soothed her. "Hello, Cocoa," she said, scratching the dog's long ears, and then closed her eyes.

Under the warmth of the dog's wet tongue licking her cheeks, Candy let the unsettling events of the day slip away. Why did the world have to be so sad, so angry? "You don't know how lucky you are," she whispered into the dog's long ears. "You can't read the newspapers. You don't understand the late television news. You're not even aware of what's happening out there." She wished she weren't either.

After a short nap and dinner, Candy retired to her room to do her homework. Later in the evening, with just a small night light shining, she propped up the scrapbook her father had given her. He had printed boldly, WORDS TO LIVE BY across the front of the album. Candy turned the pages as she often did at the end of the day. It was as if she and her father were having a visit.

Each day faithfully for as long as she could remember, her father had added a quote, pasting it or writing it inside the pages of the book. Soon the book was filled with the thoughts and feelings of many famous people.

She reread one of her favorites. "All problems become smaller if you don't dodge them, but confront them. Touch a thistle timidly and it pricks you;

grasp it boldly and its spines crumble." (William S. Halsey).

Many times, when she missed her father so much that an ache formed in her throat, she would turn the pages of the scrapbook and feel he was sending messages of help back to her through the words of all the people who had lived before.

She lay the book back on the floor and picked up her photograph album. Pictures of Halloween filled the pages. There was Linda in her pretty princess costume. She insisted on always looking her best, even on Halloween. There was Candy in a pair of her father's long underwear she had found in the attic. A flowered belt hung around her waistband.

The underwear was red, the flowers multicolored. She wore sneakers in the photograph. They were painted with many striped colors. A black top hat she had discovered in a box in the attic was set jauntily on her head. A pair of lens-free sunglasses rested on her nose. Candy's smile grew stronger as she stared at the picture, recapturing the laughter that had spread through many houses after she had knocked on their front door.

The face staring back from the photograph was so funny, with bright red circles about the cheeks. Her skinny legs were hidden by long red tights. "You have Aunt Betty's long legs and free spirit," her mother often reminded her. The long underwear disguised the part of her body Candy thought less attractive than the rest, no matter what her mother thought.

There was something haughty, something of that

free spirit in the eyes that stared back at her from the album. Later that night, lying in bed with Cocoa curled under the blanket next to her feet, Tiger on top near the pillow, Candy thought about the quote from her father's scrapbook: ". . . grasp it boldly and its spines crumble."

The months passed before her like a clock spinning out of control. Everyone around her was doing what they wanted to do: wearing sloppy clothing, throwing trash cans, breaking into lockers, taking it for granted that she would accept it.

Suddenly she sat straight up in bed, her eyes bright with excitement. She didn't have to accept it if she didn't want to. Tomorrow she could start to make all the spines crumble if she chose. And she knew just how she could do it.

2

She had almost forgotten what she intended to do when she first arose from bed. She looked out the window. It was another gray day. There was no sun rising up behind the hill in back. The trees were listless, as if they too were tired of the relentless winter.

Candy's hands drifted through the closet, past the skirts, the blouses, the slacks. Nothing interested her. Then, accidentally, she stepped on the albums, one piled atop the other . . . one filled with the quotes her father had gathered, the other with photographs from Halloween. It was as if the two had joined to send her a message. The book of quotes lay there, challenging her with its voices from the past that believed in action. She remembered last night's decision and brightened. Her heart raced as she ran into her mother's room.

"Where're my sneakers?" Her brother, Ian, called from the other room.

"Where'd you leave them?" a voice from the kitchen carried up the steps.

Candy pulled the long underwear from the bottom drawer of her mother's bureau. There were still a few old things kept there: a polka-dot tie of her father's, a pair of gloves riddled with holes from wear. The bright red of the underwear immediately cheered her up, and she giggled. She raced into her brother's room, wading through last night's clothes still heaped on the floor. Ian was kneeling on the rug, peering under the bed. His red hair fell forward.

"Did you see my sneakers?" he asked.

"I saw them downstairs behind the couch," Candy offered. "You're going to be late if you don't hurry."

Ian usually raced for the bus to junior high. "I'm not going to drive you one more time," her mother would threaten, but Ian, only son, knew her attitude would soften if the bus happened to be too quick for his short legs.

Candy opened the door which led from Ian's room into a storage area on the same level, and climbed in. It was cold in there and goose pimples ran up and down her arms as she rummaged through boxes looking for the flowered belt and striped sneakers. She found them in a plastic bag, along with sunglasses, leotards, black top hat, and small plastic bag of makeup. Even as she gathered up the articles she wondered if she really dare do it. She switched on the radio back in her room, still hesitating.

"The big news today," the radio blared, "is the rape and robbery of a woman in the subway station at Green Street."

Candy switched the station to music. The bleak news of the day shoved her toward her decision. She stood by the radio for a second, then grabbed the underwear from the bed. She'd change the big news story at Stanley High School—for the next couple of hours at least—and though it was a little late, she'd express her own opinion regarding a dress code.

The long underwear over her leotards felt warm and snug. She was well within the school's advice to wear warmer clothes. She surveyed the tall lean body in the mirror and decided her figure withstood the test of the tight clothing.

She was glad that there were no ripples of fat and that the curves appeared in just the right places. She disguised her face next, drawing wide red circles for cheeks, and dark black lashes which widened her already dark eyes. Then she sat on the edge of the bed, fussing with the long strings of the sneakers.

Ian appeared in the room, his own sneakers in his hand. "I found them," he announced jubilantly. He disappeared around the doorway but promptly returned to his former position, as if he needed a second look to believe what he had seen. "Are you kidding?" he asked, his blue eyes wide with disbelief, a finger pointing her way.

"What's wrong?" Candy sat there tying the bows of her sneakers as calmly as if she were sitting on the edge of the bed wearing the usual jeans and sweater. She tucked her wild hair under the top hat, patted it down snugly on top of her head, and marched past a gaping Ian, who stood rooted to the spot. He followed her downstairs, speechless for the first time in many a talkative morning.

"Ian." Mrs. Miller turned, exasperated, swallowing

a last gulp of orange juice, both eyes turned upward toward the kitchen clock. "I am absolutely not going to drive you to school if you miss the bus. You walk today and I mean . . ." Her last words trailed off as the figure in red underwear entered the kitchen. A smile replaced the frown on her face.

"Oh, Candy. You're wearing your old Halloween costume. I really think that was my favorite one. And the flowers. They still look so fresh and real. Now go ahead, dear, and take it off, or you'll be late too." Her mother, though a small wiry woman half Candy's size, had a surprising strength in her arms as she led Candy toward the kitchen table. "Come on now," she urged. "Have breakfast first. It's getting late."

Candy gulped the orange juice down, then filled a bowl with cold cereal and milk. "Don't worry, Mom. I am ready."

Her mother popped the toast from the toaster, misunderstanding Candy's intentions. "Well, as long as it doesn't take you long to change. I've got such a busy day ahead of me. After work, I'm going over to the senior-citizen home. It's my turn to volunteer, take some of the residents to the bank and shopping." Then her look became more determined. "I'm taking some time off today to talk with your principal about the deplorable condition of the lockers. Something must be done about that situation."

The doorbell rang. Cocoa verified it with her beagle bark. Tiger accompanied the dog to the door as if it were also her job to guard the house.

"Come in, Linda," her mother said, just as she had

on most school mornings since Linda and Candy were eight years old. Linda's home was connected to Candy's as were all the row homes on the block, each one leaning against the other. It gave Candy the feeling of closeness, of Linda's being part of her house, part of her family, always there right on the other side of the wall. Though the walls were thick and old, sometimes she could hear the faint hum of a television playing next door, or a voice rising loud enough to be heard. She never really felt alone.

Candy grabbed her books, kissing her mother on the cheek as she rushed by. She heard her say, "You're not going to school like that!" and rise in disbelief behind her as she ran down the stoop, Linda running after her.

"I know! You're pledging for that new sorority!" Linda was looking at her hopefully, as if she had just guessed the answer to the jackpot question on a quiz show.

"You know I hate sororities," Candy scolded her.

"Someone dared you to do it," Linda tried again. Her voice didn't sound as confident this time. She tried to control her giggles as she stared down at Candy's legs and the long red underwear protruding from the winter jacket. They didn't have much time to continue the discussion.

Everyone at the bus stop wanted to know the same thing. Where was she going? A party after school? What was the occasion? Candy just shrugged, letting them draw their own conclusions. She wasn't ready to tell any of them yet, not even

Linda, that her outrageous outfit was no more absurd than anything else going on at Stanley High.

Walking down the high-school corridor alone was another matter. Candy stopped in front of her locker. She felt a momentary panic, wondering if the smartest thing she could do was to change into her regular clothes and forget the whole matter.

Then she opened her locker and remembered the missing ski jacket and the old one she was now wearing. She put the faded jacket on the hook, recalling the bright red one that had been hanging there only yesterday. She deserved something better to happen this morning. She had to begin somewhere to let everyone around her know she would not accept things as they were anymore.

She threw back her shoulders, just as her mother did when she was ready to tackle something especially difficult, and walked toward her first class.

Linda's parting shot hung over her like a cloud. "Are you sure you're O.K.?" she asked doubtfully. The old concern returned to her eyes. Lately it was missing whenever Pete was around.

Candy's answer had been to tip her black top hat. But now, facing the whistles and pointing fingers, she wasn't as self-confident. "Sergeant Miller," she muttered to herself as she moved through her long first class, "you and your scrapbook."

Linda met her later in front of their English class. She leaned forward and whispered as if they were joined in some conspiracy, "Are you going to wear that outfit all day?"

"Sure. Aren't you wearing those?" She pointed to Linda's dungarees with patches on the back.

"These are different," she defended.

"So are these," Candy agreed. "You don't think it's funny now. You did when I wore them on Halloween.

The green eyes challenging hers were filled with disapproval. "That was Halloween, a long time ago. This is January. I think it's ridiculous. And so does Pete."

It was obviously Pete's disapproval that Linda was having trouble with. "Well, I think Pete is ridiculous, and he's not even wearing red underwear," Candy shot back, her words sending Linda on her way.

"Ridiculous" was not the correct word for Pete. "Dangerous" was. Since he had come into Linda's life, she had changed. Slowly, but consistently, everything about her had grown tougher, as if another layer had been added, one Candy didn't know or care to know.

It took an extra five minutes to get the science class under control after Candy entered. Mr. Marks, the science teacher, took one look at Candy and collapsed in his chair, laughing. He wiped at his eyes, recleaned his glasses, and finally had to go out to the water fountain to regain his composure.

"Candy, you're just what I needed today," he said before giving the class its assignment. Everyone around her seemed in a better mood and Candy attributed it to the bright red underwear and the yellow dandelion which a friendly passerby had donated and which now stuck up from her hat.

Later in the hall she passed Flip Davis. Though his name was Philip, no one ever dared call him that. It was always Flip, for he was constantly flipping records at parties as part of his plan to become a disc jockey. Flip stood by the water fountain, almost resting against it. He wore dungarees and his sweater was the color of his brown eyes. He had thick brown curly hair, which he tended as carefully as Candy cared for Cocoa and Tiger. Flip wasn't overly good-looking, not in the usual sense, but somehow Candy found herself always looking his way when he was around.

His long arms were constantly waving to the beat of a small portable radio he kept in his pocket or hanging from his shoulder. Now he stood chewing on a pencil thoughtfully, his eyes following her.

"Hey, legs," he called after her. "You look terrific. That underwear has class."

Her face unexpectedly turned the color of her outfit. She spun around and gave him a long—and she hoped superior—look. She tried to concentrate on disliking him. He was thin, with high cheekbones that seemed to take up most of his face. His eyes were heavy with dark circles, as if he needed a good night's sleep. Candy might have convinced herself he was a total loss except for his smile, which was warm, generous, and now turned fully her way. The smile brightened his nice brown eyes. Candy decided to toss a remark his way. "I'm glad you like it," she said, sensing his approval, feeling more secure because of it. She walked by him slowly, letting him take in the full figure under the underwear, feeling much more daring in her outfit than she had ever felt wearing a dull skirt.

Flip made a circle with his fingers in her direction, as if his approval were sealed and delivered, then went on his way, pursuing a blonde with a blouse much too small and slacks that would surely have to be cut off her body when she undressed.

Candy decided he had limited interests, one of which he was presently following. His other pastime was hanging out near the flagpole at the corner of the high-school lawn. She felt he must own the pole by now. There were usually several long-legged girls surrounding him. Loud music could be counted on from the center of the group, from the portable which was as much a part of Flip's attire as the comb constantly weaving its way about his curly brown hair.

Candy bumped into her mother on the way to history class. She pulled Candy aside. "It wasn't hard finding you today, Candy. What in the world are you up to?" .

"I'll tell you tonight," Candy promised, kissing her mother's flushed cheeks, but actually stalling for time. Perhaps by tonight she might think of a reasonable explanation.

"Well, we'll both have plenty to talk about." Her mother's shoulders straightened as she walked toward the principal's office. "I might be late," she reminded Candy. "Don't forget to drop over to Aunt Betty's. She cashes her checks today."

Every Tuesday after school Candy stayed on the bus for ten more blocks, from South Ninth Street to South Nineteenth Street, where her aunt lived. On Tuesday afternoon the hours were devoted to Aunt Betty and her shopping, banking, or whatever other errands she might need taken care of.

"I don't want her walking around that neighborhood alone," her mother always fretted.

Aunt Betty's rebuttal was usually, "Nonsense, I can take care of myself."

But Candy went on Tuesdays and Aunt Betty was always happy that she was there. "No gang's going to snatch my pocketbook away," she would declare with certainty. The terrible truth was that her seventy-year-old frame was no match for even one purse snatcher, let alone a group of them.

Candy had to stay at school later that day to retake a test. Then, on her way out, she stopped at the school newspaper office. She often did volunteer work. One of the news items spread out on the table was headlined, "Dress codelessness expands. Red underwear is in."

"You're protesting the lack of a school dress guide, aren't you?" an observant editor asked.

Candy decided this was the time to publicly announce her purpose. "Yes," she answered firmly, respecting him for being so perceptive. "Isn't it about time someone did?" The editor quickly assigned a reporter to a follow-up article rallying all those in favor of a dress guide.

Candy wanted to tell him it was more than that . . . it was the school break-ins, the vandalism in the bathrooms. It was the lack of caring about one another. But then all that seemed too much to dump on the newspaper at one time, so she left the office with their article unaltered, admitting it was a beginning, anyway.

She showed up at her aunt's row house still dressed in her red underwear. There hadn't been any time to change. Her aunt's house, joined together as was Candy's by many others, was two stories. It was the last on the block, surrounded by tall poplar trees. It was an old home, older than Candy's. Candy's mother had been born in this house, as was Aunt Betty. Her mother had married and moved with Sergeant Miller ten blocks down the avenue. Aunt Betty had remained, the home in her name. Many of the people in the neighborhood married and moved close to the same streets they had lived on while growing up. But lately Aunt Betty's block had changed drastically, with none of her former neighbors living there any longer.

Aunt Betty was sitting in the living room waiting. It appeared that all her things were waiting with her. Several grandfather clocks lined the walls. Plastic bags of assorted sizes lay bordering the room, waiting patiently to be looked into. Plants, little ones and hanging ones, some filling up the windows, left little spare room.

"My goodness, Candy! I thought the bank would close before you got here," her aunt said crossly, tucking a strand of silver-blond hair back up into a knot and grabbing her pocketbook.

Candy adored her. Even though she was always

buying odds and ends that eventually would be given or thrown away, even though it was usually Candy who would have to spend an entire Saturday uncluttering the house, only to have it cluttered again the next week, she would not have traded her aunt for any other in the entire world.

"They threw away the mold when they made her," Candy's father used to say, shaking his head every spring when he cleaned out her cellar. Now a cleaning service did it.

Secretly Candy felt they didn't quite throw away the mold. After all, wasn't she a sister free spirit to her aunt and didn't one free spirit have to protect another?

"Come on, Candy. We'll never make it before closing time."

There was no mention of the underwear or the black top hat. Aunt Betty just readjusted her glasses and pulled Candy along up the block. "You know I don't like to walk through these streets after dark."

It was the first time Candy ever heard her aunt admit she was afraid.

"You know Mr. and Mrs. Katz, that elderly couple who live down the block? They were coming from the supermarket when a big mean boy grabbed their bags and knocked them down." Aunt Betty's voice was soft, as if she were telling a bedtime story, a made-up one that wasn't quite real.

They completed their business at the bank and were just outside the front door when Candy spotted Flip with his portable, leaning against the pole that held the street sign. She wondered if he ever stood upright without his legs bent sideways in a reclining position.

"Hi." He waved.

"Hi," she answered. The underwear suddenly felt much heavier and much redder. Aunt Betty's arm grew tighter about her own. Flip's dark dungarees and jacket, along with an unexpected tough look on his face, didn't strengthen Aunt Betty's confidence.

"What are you doing over here?" he asked, walking in step with them.

"Visiting my aunt." She noticed his eyes were dark brown with yellow flecks. She wondered if it was just the sun's reflection.

"This can be a rough neighborhood," he cautioned her.

"We don't have to walk too far." She wanted to tell him she could take care of herself. And her aunt. But she decided total honesty wasn't always the best policy.

He walked along with them as if he had been invited. Aunt Betty clutched her pocketbook, now and then looking over her sunglasses at him. Finally she came to her own conclusion that he could probably be trusted and relaxed her grip on Candy.

They reached the house finally, the green curtains in the windows a welcoming sign.

"I'll let myself in." Aunt Betty hurried ahead, taking it for granted Candy would stay behind. Even though it was a cold winter afternoon, some of the neighbors sat huddled on stoop steps. Aunt Betty walked briskly past them and waved as she opened and closed the door.

Candy stood there feeling rather foolish. She had intended to go inside with her aunt and stay the rest of the afternoon. Flip's appearance had ended the day quite differently.

He took it for granted that she would walk home instead of taking the bus and that he would walk with her.

"Where's your other half? Linda?"

Candy resented his referring to her that way. "With Pete Fields, I guess."

"You mean he's out of jail?"

"He never was in," Candy said defensively, not wanting to defend Pete at all, but feeling a certain loyalty to Linda.

"Maybe I just feel he belongs there," Flip corrected himself. "Why'd you wear the outfit?" he asked, shifting subjects without warning. He was exactly her same height. It was difficult to avoid his gaze.

"Why not?" she shot back, again feeling on the defensive.

He shrugged. The lanky shoulders changed position. He had spent two of the ten blocks combing his hair. The curls remained stubbornly. The portable bobbed up and down around his shoulder. Yet there was something easy about being with him, just like putting her foot in a shoe that fit just right.

Candy was disappointed when they approached her house. There were times the walk seemed unbearably long. Today it was all too short.

"Do you visit your aunt often?" he asked.

"Usually on Tuesday," she answered. She felt as if they were arranging a date. He put the comb through the curly hair one more time. "You look good in red, kid." Again the smile and suddenly a kiss on her forehead right below the black top hat. There was an edge of possession to the kiss, as if there had been an exchange of ownership. It unnerved Candy. He moved like Tiger, her cat, quickly and without warning.

Candy ran into the house. Her mother was waiting for her as she came into the living room. Ian was sitting on the couch with her, listening.

"So I told the principal about those lockers and how they should be fixed. All of them."

"What did he say?" Ian asked.

"He said, instead of worrying about lockers, which he felt were as adequate as any lockers anywhere, I should be worrying about my daughter, who is showing up in school in long red underwear. He hopes it won't happen again."

A grin curled about Ian's face. He was always delighted to find Candy in trouble.

"He's not going to do anything about the lockers being broken into?" Candy interrupted.

Her mother stared at her, as if seeing her for the first time. "Candy, I've had a very difficult day." She straightened the pillows on the couch as if that would help matters. "All the people at the senior-citizens home are terrified to go outside. They won't shop or go to the bank. They've heard these frightening tales about older people being mugged and they're afraid to lose what little they have. It's so unfair, to pick on old people who couldn't possibly defend themselves. To rob anyone like that infuriates me. And do you know what's so unjust about it all?"

They both were thinking about Sergeant Miller now, but Candy knew neither could admit it.

"It's the young picking on the old."

The entire conversation at the dinner table returned to the locker situation.

"It's the school's responsibility to provide adequate lockers," Mrs. Miller insisted, "but the principal says he can't keep track of two thousand of them and their upkeep."

Ian was unusually silent, but now and then he cast a glance Candy's way. She knew he was aching to introduce the subject of long underwear, but a certain amount of good judgment kept him from doing it.

It was only while washing dishes that her mother referred to "that other matter," which seemed a good-enough phrase and which convinced Candy that her mother did not wish the long-underwear episode to continue.

"I'm so glad you're not going to wear that outfit anymore."

Candy felt her mother's disapproval in the tone of her voice and the frown that crossed her forehead. It was more an order than a request.

"I'm having enough trouble with the principal," she sighed, hanging up the dish towel.

That night, the scrapbook lay on the floor beside her bed as though challenging her. How could she tell her mother, Flip, Linda, or any of them that her father, somehow, in some way, was gently leading her toward what she must do. Her mother was right. She would not wear the red underwear again. To-morrow she would go to school dressed as a raisin.

3

Linda stood facing the mirror, using the morning sun as a spotlight as she examined her face. It was difficult to believe that only a couple of weeks ago, the cheeks were sore, the eyes circled with dark rings. Now all gone. As if a magic wand had waved all traces of the operation away.

Vanished. In its place was a beautiful piece of sculptured art, her new nose. Created by a talented plastic surgeon, a sixteenth-birthday gift from her parents, it was everything she had dreamed it would be. The bump was gone forever. Though the new nose slanted upward a little more than she would have liked, Linda realized it was just a matter of getting used to something different.

She sat down at her desk and combed her long strawberry-blond hair. She could hear the faint hum from Candy's radio playing on the other side of the wall. Linda glanced at the clock and realized she'd better hurry. Usually she would knock three times against the wall, letting Candy know she would meet her outside on the stoop in five minutes. This morning she didn't.

It was better this way. Their walks to school lately were no longer enjoyable. The silences were awkward, the conversation forced. Sooner or later, Pete Field's name would come up and Candy's disapproval rode over her like a herd of wild cattle. She always felt the bruises later.

"He's always in trouble," Candy would say. "He's bound to drag you into one of his skirmishes."

Linda was aware of the rumors that followed Pete, but the two months he'd been hanging around her had been without incident. Linda felt the accusations were unfair.

Quickly she reexamined the reflection in the mirror. Her hair was shining, freshly washed. It hung past her shoulders, and she was determined to let it grow until it reached her waist. She peered a little closer to the mirror, satisfied her milklike skin was free of pimples. She didn't care what Candy thought about Pete. Pete Fields was the best thing that had happened to her. When she was with him, she felt different than the old Linda, who never seemed to have anything bright to say, who followed Candy around as if there were a leash and collar about her neck.

Pete didn't care what she talked about or if she talked at all. Yet he made her feel important, the way he tucked her under his arm when they walked down the school corridor.

Linda smiled at her image in the mirror. It pleased her. For fifteen years the bump on the nose had been there to stare back at her. That's why it had been so important for her to have everyone's approval, to wear the clothes, that were popular, to style her hair the way everyone else did, to follow those who looked as if they knew where they were going. She wanted to go there with them. Pete made her feel like somebody, even by the way he walked with her, as if no one dared get in their way.

"You don't need someone like him," Candy kept saying all the time now.

Linda pinned a gold clip in her hair. Candy could not begin to understand what it was like to walk through life with something on her face that she wished weren't there. Candy loved being different. She wore skirts that no one else would touch. She'd sometimes wear dresses, looking as if she were going out on a Sunday afternoon, when all she was doing was going to school. It always seemed she was out there alone on her own island, but loving every minute. Sometimes Linda almost disliked Candy for her strength. It was always there, making Linda feel inadequate.

She caught one more glimpse of her reflection, remembering her mother's words, spoken so often when she caught Linda gazing sadly into the mirror: "Honestly, honey. You can hardly notice it. Nobody's nose is perfect." Her mother would repeat that statement day after day, as if saying it would wash away Linda's pain.

It was almost as though her mother felt guilty, producing a daughter who was dissatisfied with some part of her anatomy, perhaps even having to admit to herself that the product wasn't exactly perfect. But the words didn't wipe away what Linda

35

saw in the heart-shaped glass in front of her each day. She didn't care about other people's noses. Just about her own. Well, now her mother would not have to feel guilty any longer.

Nor would her mother have to worry about "Linda's attitude," which her parents had felt was becoming negative and inward. They were right in a way. As the years passed, she had drawn as little attention to herself as possible, closed herself off as a flower draws up its petals. Sometimes, when things grew really desperate and it was an effort to face anyone but Candy, she would walk looking down at the sidewalk, at the school floors.

But at last her parents gave in to her persistent pleas for plastic surgery. Though money was tight, the family agreed, Linda promising to pay her parents part of the money with her summer earnings. Now at last the nightmare was over.

Linda gathered her schoolbooks from her desk and ran downstairs. She wondered if it had been a mistake telling Candy and Pete not to let anyone know about the operation. The couple of weeks of Christmas vacation had provided the necessary time for healing. Only a slight redness remained. Linda wanted her classmates to discover the new Linda all by themselves. It unnerved her to admit that, as yet, hardly anyone had.

She sat down at the breakfast table. The toast and orange juice were neatly set on a plate, a napkin by the side, two vitamins and a glass of milk by their side. With an older brother away at college, most of the attention now fell on her. It was as if she had become her parents' entire occupation.

Linda heard the shower running as she hurriedly ate and slipped away from the breakfast table, eager to avoid any conversation with her mother. She didn't feel like admitting to anyone that the operation had not brought the great change she imagined.

The winter air was cold and refreshing, shaking the sleep from her body. It caught Linda by surprise. She pulled up the collar of her coat to protect the newly healed skin of her nose.

Just as she reached the corner, a motorcycle, black and soaring, pulled up, almost at her feet. All she saw were helmet, goggles, and long black pants. But there was no mistaking Pete's dark eyes from under the helmet. No one else had his boldness as he pulled up to her on the sidewalk. He slipped off the helmet. "Hop on," he ordered.

She obeyed, mounting the motorcycle as if it were a horse ready to gallop over the countryside. On the back of his motorcycle, she could be anything she dared to be, and her mind whirled with fantasies. Pete dropped her off near the school's tennis courts.

"Aren't you coming in?" she asked.

"Not today." He revved the motor and disappeared up the block as if school were just a sometime thing that he could easily do without.

Linda made her way through the halls, feeling an emptiness inside. She had always imagined herself in a relationship with a boy, and the thoughts they might share. Most of what she felt was kept carefully locked within. She wanted desperately to release it.

There had been scattered dates before Pete. But the last couple of months, he had somehow put a stamp on her, a stamp that might have read, "My property." She could not lie to herself. Pete was not the sharing kind. When it really came down to it, he really wasn't her type at all. His smile could turn mean as quickly as his eyes, dark and threatening. Sometimes when his triggerlike temper went out of control, he actually frightened her, and fascinated her at the same time. More and more she felt drawn to him. It was almost as though the more Candy disapproved, the more she felt compelled to turn his way. Candy was always telling her what to do. At eight years old, it didn't seem to matter. At sixteen, it did.

Linda opened her locker door and hung up her jacket. She let her fingers run over the smoothness of her nose as she stood sheltered by the long steel door. She stared at the picture on the inside of her locker. It was last year's class picture. There in the red dress sat the old Linda, as if she had nothing to look forward to. Sad eyes. Sad mouth. She peered closer and could see the lump, even in the photograph. Linda leaned against the locker for a moment, wondering how she could have endured looking that way all those years. She took down the photo and stuck it back in the locker.

And then her thoughts returned to Pete. She was sure the new Linda was ready for someone like him. Maybe if she was to really change, it was necessary to rid herself of all the old faces, and bring only new ones into her life.

History class was first. There was again no acknowledgment of the big change on her face. She paid particular attention to those around her. There was not a single "Ahh" or an "Oooh" or a "Look's great," to pick her spirits up. It was as if nothing had happened. The big secret had certainly been faithfully kept. But it was not the way she had imagined. It disappointed her to think the surgery might remain a secret forever.

The rest of the morning went by uneventfully. She found herself searching frantically for Candy, her self-confidence waning as the truth faced her through every class. But as often as they ordinarily met before, Candy had today become invisible. Linda knew she must be avoiding their usual meeting places; maybe Candy too felt the awkwardness in their conversations lately.

A small group of girls turned the corner. They were laughing, doubling over the books they were carrying.

"Did you see her in that outfit?" one of the group asked another.

"How does she have the nerve?" another questioned.

"I think she's flipped out," a third offered. The other heads nodded in agreement.

Linda turned the corner, only to run smack into a large object that resembled an overgrown raisin. The body was covered with dark brown burlap. For any who had difficulty guessing, a sign on the raisin's front proclaimed:

> I am a raisin,
> Don't you agree?
> The best-dressed raisin is me.

Linda took a moment to read the poem hanging from Candy's neck and then she stood back in shock. The first costume of long underwear had struck her as funny, only because she thought it was just one of Candy's stunts that wouldn't last. A flattering article in the newspaper, a little publicity, and the matter would fade along with Candy's interest. But facing Candy again in extreme costume, Linda realized Candy was doing all this for some more definite reason.

They stood face to face, Candy's dark eyes staring out from underneath a burlap hood.

"Everyone thinks you're nuts," Linda whispered, hoping not too many noticed the conversation. The eyes facing her widened, a bad sign, usually meaning Candy was ready to do battle.

"Well, I think everyone in this school is nuts." Candy pointed to a vulgar crayoned message scribbled on the wall. "You'd never catch a raisin doing *that*," she argued.

Linda couldn't tell if she were joking, but guessed from the narrowing eyes that she was not. "Do you mind telling me how long you're going to keep this up?" She almost wished Candy wouldn't tell her, for, once she did, Linda would have to decide what to do about it.

Candy suddenly turned around and it was then Linda saw the sign hanging on her back.

"All that is essential for the triumph of evil is that good men do nothing" (Edmund Burke).

"I think that quote from my scrapbook should tell you all you need to know." Candy turned around, pulling off the hood. "You want to go to lunch?" she asked.

Linda had no intention of walking down the corridors with a raisin. The long underwear had been bad enough. Linda's old insecurities came back to haunt her, and she used Pete as an excuse. "I'm meeting Pete for lunch." She told herself it was only half a lie, for Pete might well have returned to school by now.

Candy's lips tightened, as if she were making up her mind whether to continue the conversation. Linda hoped she wouldn't. Candy did.

"He's a number-one jerk and so are you for even going near him. It's only a matter of time until he gets into trouble he can't get out of."

The words made Linda's spine tingle. Her shoulders straightened. If she were ten years old again, she would have tackled Candy onto the ground and settled it instantly. But somewhere during the last six years she had lost the ability to react without caring how she looked. Instead, she found herself defending Pete, even though she wasn't certain he deserved it. "You don't even know him. How do you know what he's like?" The thought followed that maybe Candy objected to Pete because Linda was no longer her obedient partner.

"All you have to do is ask any policeman in this town," Candy hit back. Along with the insult, she jabbed twice on Linda's shoulder, like an exclamation mark at the end of a sentence.

"If you were a real friend, you'd try to get to know him." It was as if they were in a boxing tournament, each one going for the knockout punch.

The hood went back on. The raisin made an about-face and left Linda standing there, feeling angry and alone.

At the end of the day Pete was waiting by the tennis courts when she came out of the building. All her doubts about him flew away. The need not to feel alone was greater than any danger he might present.

"Where's your twin?" he asked sarcastically as he drove her home on the motorcycle.

She didn't answer his question.

"I don't think your friend likes me." He laughed as he said it. She felt it ripple through his body and connect to her own.

"We're not friends anymore," Linda answered boldly. He revved up the motorcycle and she wasn't certain if he heard, but her own announcement left her somewhat shaken. There was more truth to the statement than she would have liked.

Maybe they weren't friends anymore. Maybe they had become just a habit. If she were to be a new Linda, perhaps her first action should be to shed her old ways, and with them the old friends who no longer understood her.

She held on tightly to Pete as he sped down the street. She didn't feel daring or notice anything except when she was next to him, and she didn't want to lose that. She needed him, not for Candy's reasons, but for her own.

Later that night her hand went up several times toward the wall that separated her bedroom from Candy's. She didn't knock the three times good night as she had for so many years. In warm weather she would tap at Candy's front window with a hanger, so they could both lean out for the last-minute conversation.

She was tired of knocking, tired of always following Candy's lead. She lay awake listening for a tap at the wall from the other side. It never came.

The old Linda would have given in first. The new Linda turned on her side and went to sleep.

4

Candy stood in the girl's room in front of the large mirror, studying her costume for the day. Today she was wearing a huge white apron with a tall white chef's hat she had borrowed from the nearby Napoli restaurant. She tried to adjust the hat, which was leaning too far down in front.

She walked to the sink with the only operating faucet. The other two faucets were missing. Only a couple of years ago the bathroom had been redecorated with new sinks and large mirrors. It had taken only a short while for destruction to set in.

Candy peered closer to the mirror. It was bordered with messages from one classmate to another, some written in lipstick on the glass, other small notes stuck in the frame. Nothing to her from Linda, not that she really expected there would be. Linda had called her nuts. The image in the mirror didn't look that disturbed. Her eyes, darker and wider, looked rational. Yet she had to admit, there was a hint of excitement in them.

She certainly didn't feel "nuts." She felt the same as she had yesterday and the day before. In fact, she felt much better. The only shadow over the entire day was her mother's outburst as she had left the house this morning.

"You are absolutely not going to school like that again, no matter what your reason. Let someone else fight to change things!" Her mother had spoken with all the authority she could muster. Her shoulders appeared twice as wide as she stood in the doorway at the top of the stoop looking down at Candy. Candy saw a few shades pop up along the row of homes and a window open here and there. It was easy to overhear with the houses so close to one another. This morning the neighbors had probably received an earful from the Miller household.

Candy's sharp answer was directed at her mother and at anyone else who was listening, including her dear ex-friend Linda Tucker, wherever she might be. "I can wear anything to school I choose. Remember, we don't have a dress code anymore, so I'm not breaking any rules."

The silence she left behind gave her a small sense of victory, even though she knew she was not being fair to her mother. Her memory of her father and the things he believed in was also involved with what she was doing. Dad would not have accepted the present conditions at school. And so, neither would she. But the pain in her mother's eyes whenever her father's name was mentioned prevented Candy from including him in her explanation, or even going deeper into many of the leftover feelings that still lay unexplored between her mother and herself.

It was all Mr. Parker's fault anyway, Candy thought, letting her hands dry under the hot-air dryer. Yesterday he wore the red-striped shirt with the tight dungarees. His mustache was untrimmed and his beard, long and unkempt, still retained bits of food from the lunch hour. It repelled her to look at him. Yet there he was, wearing what he wanted to wear. There she was, having to look at it, but worse than that, having to accept it. Having to accept the toilet paper strewn across the bathroom floor and the window shade, once crisp and new, now with a slash up the middle.

She straightened the sign attached to the apron. She had picked it out carefully from her father's collection. It was one of her favorites.

"The hero is no braver than an ordinary man, but he is brave five minutes longer" (Ralph Waldo Emerson).

Before she was finished, Candy vowed, everyone around her would get the message. Stanley High was a school filled with cowards. No one dared to speak out or stand alone.

During the rest of the morning several of her classmates came over to inspect the outfit, but for the most part Candy felt a reserve around her, as if she had become isolated on an island with all those she knew standing on a far-off shore and silently watching.

Particularly Linda. They sat at the same lunch table, but not together. Linda was at one end, Candy at the other. Everyone in between sensed what was going on. It was as if an operation had

47

been performed, separating the two of them. Linda was making it very clear to all those around that they were no longer joined in thought or deed.

They were, however, thrown into each other's company again during biology lab.

"I think you're flipping out," Linda finally blurted, the frog between them in a most unglamorous pose. "Why do you want to walk around looking so weird?"

"I don't think I look weird at all," Candy answered defiantly, pushing the chef's hat back on her head. "No weirder than everyone else around here." She took her turn with the frog, not really caring to know the details of his inner body.

"Sure, everyone walks around with a sign pinned to a large apron and a hat flopping down in their eyes."

Candy concentrated on the frog. It began to hold more appeal than Linda at the moment.

"I really don't understand you at all anymore." Linda closed her notebook and moved to the other side of the table, as if Candy had some contagious disease.

"Maybe you never did." Candy tucked some wisps of hair back under the hat, trying to hide the hurt she felt facing Linda's rejection. She couldn't tell Linda what was in her heart, for a wall had sprung up between them that made trust impossible. They no longer knew each other as they once had. It was as if they had both just moved into the neighborhood.

But what had happened to all the past years they

had collected? Hadn't she seen Linda through the long-ago episode of the screechy pop-up toaster, when Linda would run out of the kitchen every time someone made a piece of toast? Hadn't Linda's mother even moved the toaster into the dining room? No one called Linda nuts then, though Candy often stared at the toaster, wondering what was so nerve-shattering about it. But she had never thought Linda was flipping out. She had accepted her friend the way she was. One day, without explanation, Linda moved the toaster back into the kitchen. Nothing was said about it again. She might just bring up that toaster matter if Linda called her nuts again.

Candy ran into her English class just before the bell rang. Her teacher, Mr. Smith, handed her a note accompanied with a frown. "I think the guidance counselor would like to see you," he said softly.

On her way with some trepidation to the counselor's office, Candy passed the library, where a piece of cardboard was pasted over the front of the broken door window. She poked her head through the open door and waved to the librarian. Her reward was the laughter she heard as she passed by. But that broken window was another result of the recurring school vandalism. Perhaps she might also be able to do something about that. Everything seemed to be working into one enormous project. She wondered if she were really capable of handling it all.

Mr. Motts, the guidance counselor, sat at his office desk waiting. Their meetings, though infrequent, were usually pleasant. Candy had most recently dropped in to discuss possible plans for college. Though she was currently in her junior year, there were many arrangements to be made and application forms to fill out. Today Mr. Motts had a strained expression on his face. She had never seen him wear this look before, but suspected it was reserved for students in trouble.

She sat down on the soft leather chair opposite him, carefully adjusting the sign on her apron. She straightened the chef's hat and smiled. Mr. Motts looked as if he were trying not to smile back. She watched his mouth curl in a grin, then tighten as self-control won out. He cleared his throat and shuffled some papers on his desk. He reminded her of her father when he used to sit down to work on the bills each month. It was a job he didn't look forward to.

"Candy," Mr. Motts began in a firm voice, "I called you down here because . . ." He paused, raising the pencil which now pointed toward her. "Because of that . . ." The pencil pointed first toward her hat, then gradually found its way toward her apron. "Your outfit." His mouth softened, then regained control.

Candy was surprised at her own reaction of shock. What had she really expected? When she allowed herself to face reality this past week, she knew the faculty would not accept her behavior for long. While Mr. Motts seemed determined to explain his position, Candy's eyes lingered on the space between his shoes and the cuff of his trousers. He wore no socks.

"The first day, well, you know, the long red underwear . . . we all thought it was funny and a very cute original idea. The school newspaper article explained your position and that was fine." He took off his eyeglasses and wiped them clean, searching for the proper words. "However, we think this has gone far enough, Candy. You're disrupting classes and we can't have that."

It wasn't true. They accepted disruption every day. Students were always shouting back at the teachers. Was she disrupting things any more than the punk who threw the wastebasket across the room or the ones who smoked pot in the back of the room where everyone could smell it and know it and have to accept it?

"Except for some laughter, and that only lasted a couple of minutes, I haven't noticed any difference in the classrooms." Candy felt it was time to begin her defense.

Mr. Motts rose from his chair and walked around the room. Candy watched his pale white ankles appear and disappear beneath his trousers.

"Look, just what do you hope to accomplish by this outlandish behavior?"

"There's no dress guide in our school handbook," Candy reminded him. "In fact, we don't seem to have many rules about anything." She still remembered her father's words when she was very small and sitting on his knee: "Without rules, Candy, innocent people get hurt."

Mr. Motts' eyebrows arched and Candy wondered if she had gone too far. She never answered her teachers back, certainly not with belligerence, not like many of her classmates who heckled the teachers, were sent to the principal, reported to the parents, then returned to the classroom to begin heckling again.

"That's true," Mr. Motts answered, scratching his bare ankle. "But all of us try to dress within reason."

Candy wanted to ask him why he wasn't wearing socks and where his own reason began.

"Look, why don't we bring this to a close nicely?" he suggested. "I really don't believe that one person desiring a dress guide is going to make the difference. You've had your fun. We've all had a good laugh. Everyone knows where you stand. Tomorrow, please show up dressed normally. I'm sure you don't really want this situation to get out of hand."

She thought about her stolen ski jacket. Surely things were out of hand already. Could she be the only one to think so?

Mr. Motts put the papers on his desk in the file drawer, took off his eyeglasses, and stood up. The interview was over. Candy's face crumpled as she left the room. The brave front she had put on in front of Mr. Motts hid trembling hands and a nervous growling in her stomach. Mr. Motts didn't believe one person could make a difference. If she believed that, then perhaps her father's life hadn't mattered either, or the values he held, or the reason he died. Just because he cared about another human being.

Candy's eyes were blurred with tears. She bumped into Flip as she ran down the corridor. He was wearing a light green sweater and overalls. His lean body hurried after her, the portable radio swinging from his shoulders.

"Are you O.K.?" he asked. She felt his hand on her arm, then around her shoulder.

"I think so." Her mouth felt dry and tight, the way it usually felt just before a crying spell.

"What did Motts want?" Flip pulled her hat playfully. It brought her to a halt.

"Please be careful," she ordered. "It's only barely pinned on." She started forward again. She was in no mood to answer his questions, especially when the answers were out of reach.

She felt the hat tug again. "Will you let go?" Candy ordered hotly, but Flip held on stubbornly.

"I'll let go when you stop and talk to me. You're in trouble with Motts, aren't you?" he asked, finally releasing his fingers from the hat.

"Mr. Motts told me to stop wearing these outfits."

"What are you trying to prove by wearing them?" He faced her squarely now, without the usual music blaring from his shoulder. There was something about the way he asked, different than Linda's belligerent tone, that encouraged her to give him an honest answer.

"There's just a small group in this school who rules all of us, by what they do, by what they wear, even by what they think. I want to try to bring back the dress guide, and maybe a few other rules. That's the last ski jacket anyone's going to steal from my locker."

She waited for him to reject her ideas the way everyone else had, but instead he put his arm around

53

her waist and walked her to the next class. It was what he didn't say that mattered. It didn't seem to bother him to be seen with her, the way it annoyed Linda. Candy needed someone's support now and accepted Flip's eagerly, though he would have been the last she expected help from.

She ate lunch alone. Flip had a later lunch hour. Linda was nowhere around. No one else was eager to move to her table. Now and then she heard a whisper from behind.

Bill Nixon, the editor of the newspaper, caught up with her just as she was leaving school.

"Candy," he said, pulling her aside secretively as if he were a detective on the brink of solving a crime. "We're going to start a series on bringing back the dress guide. Just keep wearing those getups for a little while longer. It's just what we need to make the series catch reader interest. There are lots of us who'd like to see the school get its act together."

"Well, to tell you the truth," she began, and she was about to tell him about her fair-weather friend Linda Tucker and Mr. Motts and his bare ankles, and even about her mother, who was probably waiting for her now with the rest of what she was saving up from this morning, when Bill suddenly kissed her on the cheek and said, "You're terrific."

A flashbulb momentarily blinded Candy after Bill pulled up his camera and captured a startled chef for all his readers. He left her there as if their meeting had been a success. Candy didn't feel so terrific about it. If she were to continue these whacky disguises, Mr. Motts would have to be reckoned with.

Part of the way home, Candy thought about Mr. Motts. The remainder of the time was taken up with thoughts about Linda and the things she would say to her if they ever started speaking again. Along with the toaster, she might also have to mention the year Linda threw up every time she had to give a report in front of the class, or the habit she had of lining her shoes in a row in front of the bed, each in pairs, neatly, every night without fail. Of course, Linda might retaliate and mention the year some Indians had come to school for an assembly program and Candy had to hold her hands over her ears to keep from screaming at the sound of the tom-toms. Knowing her so well, she might even bring lots of similar incidents. Perhaps, she decided, it was better to let the past stay forgotten.

"So, how did it go today?" her mother asked as Candy entered the house. Her smile was friendly enough. Candy breathed a sigh of relief. She didn't have the strength for another confrontation.

"Well, I received a great mark on my English test. I might pull off an A." She left out Mr. Motts and tried for a change of subject. "Anything new on the lockers?"

Her mother brought a bowl of fresh peas to the table and Candy sat down to help shell them. "Not really. The principal says he can't have security guards all over the place. He says everyone should keep their valuables on them. I told him everyone has to wear a heavy coat or jacket to school in the winter. He told me he had your locker fixed, but he couldn't go around fixing all of them. Most of them are in deplorable condition. However, I have no intention of giving up."

"I don't think it's reasonable that I have to be afraid to put a good jacket in my locker," Candy said, tasting a crisp uncooked pea.

"Neither do I," her mother agreed.

Candy felt her father's presence more than ever at the table while the two of them talked. She wanted to tell her mother about her feeling, but she also didn't want to be responsible for bringing that pained look back into her face . . . and all those old memories.

Instead, Candy got up and washed the raw peas in the bowl.

Later that night, she returned to her father's book of quotes.

"Where do we go now, Dad?" she asked softly, as if they were having a quiet conversation together.

Her eyes trailed across the open page before her. The answer was staring back at her in a quote from William Jennings Bryan:

Cast Your Vote

Never be afraid to stand with the minority when the minority is right, for the minority which is right will one day be the majority; always be afraid to stand with the majority which is wrong, for the majority which is wrong will one day be the minority.

Candy copied the words of wisdom carefully on a piece of paper and smiled. She added to it: "Let's bring back the dress guide and some rules of conduct." Then she proudly signed her own name, Candy Miller.

She got out of bed and took the sewing box from the bottom of her closet. Candy smiled contentedly as she threaded the needle and began to sew together her new outfit. It was not the time to give up now. Rather, it was urgent that she keep on fighting, that she and Sergeant Miller not surrender.

5

Candy banged the nails into her Aunt Betty's kitchen windows, hoping it would make the place more secure. She again checked the bolt on the front door. The lock was new, but the door was old and worn. A couple strong wrenches with a crowbar and it still might come off the hinges.

"Everything seems O.K., Aunt Betty," she called out. There was no answer from the living room, where she had left her aunt. Candy glanced about the house, still somewhat unsatisfied with her work. Her mother was constantly observing that they had "to make that place safe," always adding, "I don't know why she insists on living there alone." For a short time after Candy's father died it was expected that Aunt Betty would move in with them.

"There's no room for two women in one kitchen," was Aunt Betty's blunt reply.

Candy glanced outside. It was a beautiful Saturday, cold and crisp. The temperature hung at one degree all week and the air had a bite to it because of the extreme cold. Candy thought Flip might come over before she left this morning. "Busy Saturday?"

he had asked, calling from his office next to the pole outside the front entrance of the school. She had nodded no, thinking he meant to make her busy. But no call followed.

She wished she had called him. She thought about it. Many of the girls in school would have. But she held back. Brave about so many other decisions, she lacked the courage to go after Flip. She wasn't sure what she would do if he rejected her.

Candy put the tools away in the toolbox under the dining-room table where Aunt Betty also kept two fake plants that "I don't know where to put," and half a dozen shoes still in shoe boxes "that don't fit into my closet upstairs."

There was a hole in the rug. Candy wondered if she should talk to Aunt Betty about repairing it. She worried about her aunt and the little heels she insisted on wearing, along with the swooping skirts. She remembered as a little girl crawling under the big dining-room table when the family's dinners grew too long. She would hide amid the knees of her aunts and uncles. There had been many knees then. Her mother had two brothers and three sisters. Candy's mother was the youngest. Some had moved away to the other end of the country. Others had died. Only Aunt Betty remained close by. They treasured her like a fragile piece of fine glass that one was afraid to touch too much for fear it would break.

The house had been the family house, first owned by Candy's grandmother, then Aunt Betty, who remained the only unmarried sister. She had lived in the house all her seventy years, and knew no other place to live. The neighborhood gradually changed. Many of the corner stores closed because of repeated robberies. Old friends either died or moved away. The houses, once straight and tall in a bright new neighborhood, now appeared unsure of themselves. Though the paint was fresh on Aunt Betty's row home, it would need a scraping soon. A new roof would have to be put on. But of all the houses on the block, Aunt Betty's was the brightest.

Candy was proud of that, of the green curtains in the window, the green trim around the windowsills and on the door. The clean white steps that Aunt Betty swept constantly, the green-and-white awning hanging out over the living-room windows brought new life to the street. Whenever anyone was directed to Aunt Betty's house, they would just say, "the end house with all the green things."

Candy went into the living room and followed the sounds of something hitting the floor, coming from the kitchen. There sat Aunt Betty on the kitchen floor, legs tucked under, each other, a blue stick in her hand, with dozens of similar sticks in a circle about her.

"Pick-up sticks," she exclaimed, as if she had discovered a new toy. "Imagine finding this old box in that suitcase." She pointed to a tattered suitcase next to the kitchen cabinet, by the cellar steps. Her eyes never left the sticks scattered on the floor in front of her, the blue stick attempting to lift a yellow one off the back of a purple piece of wood.

Without looking up, for to do that would have

broken her concentration, she handed Candy a red stick.

"I used to be a champion player," she confided proudly. "Come." She patted the spot next to her. "I was always an expert at this," she boasted, skillfully lifting the yellow stick while not moving the purple stick one flutter.

"There," she said with a flush of victory brightening the blue eyes and turning the cheeks rosy. "It's your turn."

Candy took the red stick and cautiously approached a bright green one which seemed far enough away from all the others to pluck from the group. She did so successfully, but noticed her aunt's disapproval.

"Those are the easy ones," Aunt Betty said, her mouth puckering thoughtfully as she took the blue stick and popped up a green one off the back of a red one without moving the red stick at all. "Now, that's playing pick-up sticks," she shouted with the joy of a child.

Finally after much maneuvering, a stick slipped and it was Candy's turn again. The two picked up sticks for the rest of the afternoon, with much of the work yet to be done waiting patiently on the sidelines. This was the way Saturdays often went. Aunt Betty was a master at passing the hours having fun.

"Don't you just love these?" she asked, having put the sticks back in the tin can and now tucking a fake rose in her silver-blond hair, which, strangely enough, never turned gray. The rose came from a large paper bag near the tin cabinet. A little-girl smile framed her face as she unwrapped a dozen more flowers, putting a yellow one in the rubber band that held Candy's hair back in a ponytail.

"What are you going to do with all of these?" Candy asked.

"Give them away as gifts, silly. Don't they make you happy, just to look at them?"

They did. The bright colors gave Candy the same feeling she had when autumn first turned the maple trees near school bright red.

"Gifts, my dear, gifts." Aunt Betty clicked by in her shiny black shoes. "I always like to be prepared for birthdays and weddings," the voice trailed off as the silver head bent back down into the paper bag. When she reappeared, it was with several gold chains draped about her long slender fingers.

"Aren't these beautiful? I'll show you my special one."

They all looked alike to Candy, each long and thin, a single strand that could be worn about the neck. Aunt Betty lifted one chain from all the others.

"Look at this one," she instructed Candy.

Candy studied the chain closely, then shrugged. "I don't see anything different about it," she had to admit. She waited patiently for an explanation, knowing Aunt Betty liked to make a game out of everything.

Aunt Betty stretched the chain out in Candy's hands. "Most people don't see the difference. You really have to know it's there. See"—a slender finger pointed to a cluster of links—"ten of these links are round while all the others are square."

63

It was true. Now Candy could see the difference.

"This was given to me by an old beau many years ago," Aunt Betty explained. "I accidentally broke some of the links and my boyfriend had it fixed for me. We broke off soon after and I put the chain away in a box. Only years later did I take it out and notice the jeweler's mistake."

Candy wondered about the beau who had placed the chain in Aunt Betty's hands, but she knew better than to ask. Her aunt kept such things to herself.

Candy lost interest in the bag, which appeared bottomless. She drifted over to the kitchen window that faced the backyard. It was a small patch of land with a rickety wooden fence around it. There were many thick bushes, and a wide willow tree cast a heavy shadow. As Candy peered into the darkness, her eyes straining, her mother's warning came back to her. "We must convince Betty to move into a senior-citizens home. She's not safe in that house alone. See what you can do."

No one was closer to Aunt Betty than Candy. Her mother was counting on that. Suddenly the backyard looked foreboding, even treacherous. Someone stalking her aunt's house could easily find refuge in those bushes, slip past the back porch, and gain entry through a first-floor window. "They just broke into the house next door to her," her mother had warned. "It's only a matter of time."

Candy glanced over the first-floor kitchen window. Though bolstered by nails, the frames were weak and would not withstand force. Her father had trained Candy to observe such details in her own home and had trained her well. She tried to push away the warning. "It's only a matter of time."

Candy's mother was correct about the robberies. But Candy didn't agree that the solution for Aunt Betty was to leave the house she had lived in all her years and move into a senior-citizens home. She didn't even want to think of it. The idea of bringing the subject up to her aunt was more frightening than the dark grounds behind the house.

Candy took a cookie from the cookie jar that always sat on the kitchen table on top of a brightly checkered tablecloth. The kitchen was cluttered, as if Aunt Betty had just entertained. Teacups set on the table waiting, and a cake covered by a plastic cover accompanied the dishes. Aunt Betty had many friends who kept in touch by telephone, but few were well enough to visit. Still, she prepared as if they would be coming any day now.

"Could you help me?" her aunt called from the upstairs bedroom.

Candy took a quick look out the front window, hoping to see a sign of Flip's long frame, but the street was empty. She ran up the flight of steps, which creaked under her feet. The brass bed with the two swans for bedposts sat regally in the center of the room. It had been in the family for years. Candy remembered sleeping in it as a little girl and spending the entire night, eyes wide open, keeping an eye on the swans.

Her aunt was on her knees, her arms stretching into a tall bin that sat in the corner. "I want to check some items over." She pointed to the bottom of the bin.

Candy had never been in the bin before. It was one of the few places Aunt Betty avoided when they cleaned. Candy reached in and lugged some heavy plastic bags to the center of the floor.

"Go ahead. Go inside and take out the rest of the jars," Aunt Betty instructed.

Candy reached into the bin again and in the back, in the corner, were several large pickle jars. They were filled with coins. Candy brought the jars to the center of the floor.

Aunt Betty plunged her hand into her pocket and deposited some more coins into the jars. There was a jar filled with half-dollars, and one with silver dollars. The largest jar held pennies.

"Aunt Betty, you should put this money in the bank," Candy warned. "It's not safe here."

"Well, young lady, I remember when it wasn't safe in the bank. Remember, I lived during the Depression. One day I went to the bank and it was closed. All my money was gone. There's no place safer than my home." She tucked a hairpin under the bun. "Now just put those bags back, please, Candy."

Candy wondered if her aunt was aware of the break-in next door. Word must have traveled back to her. Was she just pretending it didn't happen? Was this her way of running from her own fears?

"You shouldn't keep money around like this, Aunt Betty," Candy persisted. "You don't have any more, do you?"

The blue eyes twinkled back at her as if they held a special secret. "Of course I do," she confided. "All over the place. Come with me."

They visited the cookie jar. Underneath the cookies was a piece of aluminum foil and underneath that were two ten-dollar bills neatly folded in half. They visited drawers, couch pillows, tops of shelves. Money was distributed all over the place.

Candy almost wished she hadn't seen the money. She knew it was information she should bring back to her mother, for her aunt's own safety, and yet she knew it might also be one more reason added to all the others in behalf of Aunt Betty leaving the house she loved. She didn't want to be responsible for that in any way.

The doorbell rang and Candy opened the door to Flip's smiling face. The smile was there, so easily stretching across the bony cheeks, warming the chilliest of days. She had grown accustomed to the excitement in his eyes and to the body that always moved to a musical beat of its own.

"Want to walk up the avenue?" he asked, sticking his head in the doorway.

Candy's dark thoughts vanished. She noticed that he had a dimple in his chin and his hands were muscular. Strong. Before long, she felt them about her waist.

He stepped into the living room, his eyes widening as he looked around at Aunt Betty's collection of shopping sprees.

"Do you have to clean all this up today?" he asked.

"No. I just hoped I might get some of it organized." Candy had to admit that even that appeared impossible to do. Besides, Aunt Betty didn't seem in the mood to organize.

"How come you're not dressed as a helpful elf?" he joked, pulling her dark ponytail, which swung down past her shoulders.

It felt good being in jeans and a sweater. He was referring to the costumes she now wore several times a week to school. The Bring Back a Grooming Code Committee was in full swing, with Candy providing the inspiration. The tension in the school was mounting, along with Mr. Motts' temper. Candy herself was tiring of wearing disguises that were far from flattering. Today was Saturday and she didn't want to be reminded of it.

"Oh, I'm glad you're here," Aunt Betty broke into the conversation, her white sunglasses neatly in place, though the day was cloudy. She handed Candy a triangle and a pair of sticks while she held a tambourine.

"Hi, Aunt Betty." Flip put his arm about her shoulder protectively. Candy admired the warm way he came into someone's life, as if he had always been there. It took her much longer to feel at home.

Aunt Betty smiled his way, obviously approving of his visit. She slipped her sunglasses down her nose and asked, "You wouldn't be able to play the piano, would you?"

"By ear," Flip offered.

"I just knew it." Aunt Betty clapped her hands

and led Flip to the old upright piano with a dozen plants resting on the top of it.

"Now you can both help me practice. Just sit there and hit those two sticks together, Candy, and I'll shake this old tambourine. Flip"—she patted his shoulder with the tambourine—"you hold up the melody on the piano. Our center's band will be playing in an exhibition next week and I want us to be terrific. Newspaper photographers will be there. We'll be playing 'When the Saints Come Marching In.'" She began to hum so that Flip could pick up the tune.

Candy admired Aunt Betty's devotion to the Senior Citizen Center. Each day the bus would come by her corner at eight-thirty to pick her up. At four o'clock it would deliver her back to her home. Daily, her aunt would call Candy's house to share the news of the day.

"We decorated seashells for Christmas gifts," she would share. "Next week we'll begin quilting."

But today Candy did not feel like being part of the center's band or Aunt Betty's rehearsal. She would rather have left with Flip and walked up the avenue. That was the great part about living off the main street. Hoagie shops, ice-skating rinks, movie houses, bowling lanes. There were so many ways to spend a Saturday right within their reach. Sometimes she and Linda, the thought nagged at her like a toothache, would walk up and down the avenue just peeking into stores. A bag of licorice would last the route.

She missed those walks with Linda and wondered

if they would ever share them again. She knew she couldn't blame Pete Fields for all of it. The crack in their friendship had come from more than one blow . . . perhaps many little ones added up. During the past year, without either realizing it, they had begun to concentrate on each other's faults.

Candy looked longingly toward the door, but Flip had forgotten his invitation. He was hunched over the piano, warming his fingers to the keys.

"Now, Candy, concentrate. You're not concentrating." Aunt Betty's hand went up in the air as conductor. "When I lower my hand, you both begin."

Candy sat hitting the triangle each time Aunt Betty pointed her way. Flip was really putting himself into his assignment. Her aunt's old upright had not had such a workout in many years. It appeared to be waiting for just such an opportunity, as was Flip.

"I don't have a piano right now," he confided to her aunt as if they were old friends. "I go to Uncle Jake's down the block to play his."

Aunt Betty nodded in understanding, keeping the beat of the music. She shook the tambourine gustily, her cheeks flushed. "You come over here anytime you feel the urge to play the piano," she instructed.

Flip sang along with the music. Candy relaxed.

"Candy, hit those sticks," her aunt directed, giving the tambourine a whack against her hip.

Flip's clear voice rang out above the piano. She watched his shoulders sway to the rhythm of the song. Though the room soon filled with music and laughter, there was a part of Candy that could not rise to the occasion. Even as she watched Flip at the piano, she knew there were twenty dollars hidden in the piano bench on which he sat. She realized she would somehow have to convince Aunt Betty to put all the money in the bank. She tried not to think ahead, should that attempt fail. Instead, she concentrated on the mound of brown hair and the long arms dominating the piano. By his quick acceptance of Aunt Betty and her needs, Flip had worked his way deeply into Candy's life and into her heart as well.

"I'm going to make us something to eat," Aunt Betty said after a thirty-minute workout.

Candy walked over to the piano bench and sat down next to Flip. She felt his wiry body lean toward her. The aroma of his aftershave lotion floated in her direction. It was as if he had just come out of the shower. His arm slid about her waist. The piano playing came to a sudden halt.

They turned to each other on the bench, knees pressed against one another, arms about each other's shoulders, and though it was awkward and needed some expert guidance, they found each other's lips.

She had never known such contentment before. It was as if she had reached a destination she didn't even know she was looking for. It was the same feeling she had when she would come running toward Aunt Betty's house and see the green curtains. Or when she came home after school, maybe during a snowstorm, and the house felt as if it had been waiting for her. Just right.

It all felt just right now. The shadows fell away. Except when Aunt Betty walked back in the room with the cookie jar on a tray. Candy knew it held more than cookies.

6

The bus had broken down, but that didn't much surprise Aunt Betty. The buses that took them back and forth from the Senior Citizen Center were as old and decrepit as the passengers. The center had applied for additional funds, but papers needed to be processed and all that took time.

Instead of it being four o'clock when she reached her home, it was now six-thirty and darkness towered over the street. Aunt Betty fumbled around at the bottom of her large pocketbook for her keys. Finally she felt the jagged edges, then the soft rabbit tail of the key chain. Candy had given the key chain to her with the warning, "Always have your keys in your hand when you're ready to enter your house."

There had been other warnings. "Secure your home with quality locks on door and windows." Candy had a habit of nagging. "Take care of your keys. Don't give others a chance to duplicate them." Aunt Betty could only smile now, for Candy was surely growing more like her father every day. He'd be proud of that.

She struggled with the big shopping bag and her

pocketbook, finally deciding to deposit both on the stoop while she worked at the lock, which had always been a bit stubborn. The latest campaign was to convince her to get a light timer, one that would be set to turn on automatically in the house when it grew dark outside. She didn't much see the sense of it. She rarely stayed away overnight. Still, she had to admit, standing there in front of the darkened windows, it would have been most comforting to come home to a brightly lit house.

At last the lock gave way and Aunt Betty lifted her bags. She worked her way through the doorway. Sometimes Candy persisted so with her crime-prevention lists that she almost succeeded in frightening Betty. But then she realized, Candy was a policeman's daughter and Sergeant Miller had trained her well.

For instance, now, she shouldn't have felt uneasy, walking into her own home, and yet she did. Very uneasy. She blamed Candy for that. Betty turned on the small hall light, then hung up her coat in the hall closet. She placed her wool hat on the shelf. The house felt unusually cold and damp.

"Must be that old heater again," she muttered, rubbing her hands together as she walked toward the kitchen. "What I need is a cup of hot tea to take the chill away." She often spoke aloud to herself in the empty house. The house had a way of answering her. She had grown accustomed to its creaks and drafts and leaks. They had grown old together.

Betty felt along the wall for the kitchen light. The next few moments would forever be a blur in her memory. The light spread about the kitchen. It was then, in the moment her eyes became accustomed to the brightness, that she saw the open window, actually a broken one, for there was glass scattered all about the floor.

"Oh, my." Her fingers fluttered up to her face as a sense of danger overcame her.

"Candy," she called, automatically reaching for the telephone hanging on the nearby wall. A hand closed over her own, wrenching the telephone away and placing it back on the receiver. She tried to turn to catch a glimpse of the face belonging to the body that was now in charge of her own. But failed.

An arm was about her waist, lifting her easily in the air. A hand went over her mouth as she struggled against the arms now half-dragging her into the living room. She loosened one hand and managed to fling it against the fingers about her mouth, but her strength was no match for the hands that set her roughly down on the chair.

There were two, she could judge that now. While one tied a rag about her eyes, the other tied her arms and legs with a rope. They needn't have tried so hard to keep her still, for suddenly her legs felt so weak she doubted that fleeing would have been possible.

"Did she see us? Did she see us?" one kept asking. His voice was unsure, and very young.

"Don't worry," the rougher voice assured him. "She's so old, she probably can't see anyone."

The remark was cruel and cut through Betty's terror.

"We can't let her identify us." The frightened one's voice was closer to her. She wanted to reach out, to touch him, to assure him she would protect his safety if only they would protect hers.

A hand grabbed her own and roughly pulled the jade ring off her finger. It had been a present from Candy's father. The ring came with a set of jade earrings. They were pulled from her ears.

Oh, if Sergeant Miller were here, Aunt Betty thought, struggling against the chair, her heart quickening. Perspiration dotted her forehead though the wind still blew in through the open kitchen window and throughout the house.

Was it seconds? Minutes? Had hours passed? Did she lose consciousness for a moment as the blindfold was tightened about her eyes? There was a sharp tug around her neck. The gold chain slipped away, and so did many of the memories from the past.

A voice rose against the wild beating of her heart.

"This house is loaded with stuff," the weak one said.

She had now identified him that way.

"I told you it would be," the ruthless one answered. He sounded older.

How did he know what was inside the house? Through the fog of confusion and fear, Betty forced herself to remember details of what they said to each other, the sound of their voices. Perhaps she might have the chance to identify them. If . . . the word hung over her and her body began to tremble. What if they were thinking the same thing?

What if they had no intention of letting her identify anyone?

She could hear the drawers being opened, then emptied, crashing to the floor. Indignation blotted out the panic. How dare they violate her house? Possessions, all her dear possessions, everything in their control, even her life.

She heard feet running upstairs, echoing across the bedroom overhead. Again, the sound of glass crashing—a mirror perhaps. Why did they have to do this? Steal. Destroy. Did she know them? Had they been watching her?

Betty's mind drifted as if what was happening was too painful to bear. A weightlessness invaded her body and almost felt as though she had fallen asleep.

Suddenly they were back in the room. It was as if she'd awakened from a nap and was abruptly lurched forward onto the floor. She felt their presence even before they spoke.

"I don't know if we should leave this old bag alive."

Her indignation was replaced by an urgency to convince them it was perfectly all right to leave her alive. She would promise to be good. She wouldn't tell a soul, if they would only let her live. She felt as if she were standing blindfolded before a jury.

"Feel this, lady."

Betty felt something cold and sharp pressed against her neck. It dug into her skin lightly. She tried to sit upright, perfectly still, so her skin wouldn't fold further into the object.

"It's a sharp knife, lady. All I have to do is press it." It was the ruthless one speaking now.

The weak one was in front of her also. "I don't want to get mixed up in anything like that," he said.

There was a long moment of silence. A decision was being made. Then the ruthless one withdrew the knife.

Betty felt the perspiration run down her forehead. Even the rag about her head was wet.

"Hey, if you keep it up, you'll scare her to death," the weak one cautioned. His voice was calling from the back of the house, she estimated, more toward the kitchen. Were they ready to leave?

"I need help with this stuff," the young one called again.

She was alone. She heard bags being dragged across the floor. Glasses. Coins. She heard the sound of silverware. It shouldn't matter. Next to her life, nothing should. And yet her possessions were part of her existence.

More movement throughout the house. Time was lost. Betty felt weaker, as if she had run about the block several times. Her legs began to shake. Her eyes burned. The phone rang.

"I'm here. I'm here," she wanted to cry out. But her words were locked behind the gag. It must be Candy calling. She always called about dinnertime. Was it seven? Later? Would Candy get suspicious if no one answered? Certainly she would begin to wonder.

"Come on. Hurry up," the young voice urged. His

voice sounded strained, frightened. "Someone might be coming over."

"I told you she lives alone."

How did he know so much about her? She knew nothing about them. What had made them pick her out? Had they been watching her house for a long time? Did they know what time she came home from the center?

More rustling about, and then, "What if she saw us?" The rougher one had doubts. "Hey, old lady, you goin' to talk?" The piece of metal was again at her throat.

Betty shook her head no.

There was something funny about her answer. It made him laugh, but the laugh was full of hate. Why? What had she done wrong that he hated her so?

The telephone rang again and kept ringing. For the moment it comforted her. Someone on the other end was not giving up.

The older voice was behind her now. "It's too cold in here, lady. I think we should warm it up a little for you. Hey, lady, we're going to heat up the place so you don't catch a cold."

A rustling of paper, then footsteps and laughter traveling past the kitchen, out toward the backyard.

Then silence. Just the ticking of the large grandfather clock in the hallway. For a moment Betty felt nothing but relief and a strange sense of exhilaration. She was alive. They were gone. The danger was over. Surely someone would discover her soon.

But then a strange odor penetrated the cloth

about her face. The fear she experienced before was nothing compared to the panic that gripped her. The smell of smoke drifted past her and, with it, the crackling of fire.

Frantically she moved back and forth in the chair, tipping it one way, then another, trying to loosen the ropes about her hands, scraping them as she fought for her freedom.

Finally she could battle no more. She wanted to leave this room, to drift away to another place, to run from the cruel laughter that only moments before had been behind her. The smoke was thicker. She felt herself slipping into a haze, away from the fear, away from the terrifying sounds of flames.

Gentle hands about her brought her back. This time the arms and fingers touching her were comforting and soft. Someone was untying the rope.

Mrs. Majinski's voice was soothing. "It's O.K., Betty. You're O.K. We're here now."

The blindfold was removed. At first everything blended together, but after a few moments Betty could distinguish Mrs. Majinski's face, her round shocked eyes, tears streaming down her cheeks, her hand wiping Betty's forehead while she wiped away her own grief.

"I heard the noise," she was explaining, "boys laughing in your backyard. I looked out the window and in the moonlight I could see them dragging large plastic bags."

A policeman stood at the doorway, another was kneeling beside her.

"Just a question or two," he asked gently. "How many were there?"

"Two." Her lips felt heavy, difficult to manage.

"Did you get a look at them?"

Betty managed to shake her head no. The room spun around. She grabbed on to Mrs. Majinski.

"You're O.K., ma'am. You're safe now," the policeman reassured her.

She wanted to tell him she would never feel safe again. They had taken that also, not only her belongings, but her sense of trust and security. But the words stayed behind a tongue that felt parched and stiff.

Betty wanted to tell him more, about the cruel voice and the young one, but her body was shaking now, as if it were caught in an earthquake. Mrs. Majinski held her tightly.

"It's O.K., Betty. Thank God I saw them. They had started a fire in the trash bucket."

It was only then that Betty's eyes focused on the room, and on the burned-out trash can by the desk. The living room looked as if it had been beaten up. The bags, once filled with possible presents, were empty. Some of the gifts, as if rejected, were strewn on the floor. Wrapping paper lay scattered about in balls as if there had been a party. Drawers from the dining-room buffet were standing on end in the center of the room, their contents spilled out. A lamp was overturned, another broken.

Someone handed Betty a drink of water. The small group around her had grown. A doctor—at least she concluded he was one—took her pulse. She wanted to wave him away, to assure him that she was just fine, but the words wouldn't come. In fact, she discovered she couldn't even wave him away. Though she wanted to raise her hand, oddly enough it wouldn't listen to the messages she was sending it. It remained stubbornly on her lap as if it had a mind of its own and knew better what it should do.

A stretcher was brought into the room. Mrs. Majinski was crying as she spoke to the policeman.

"Any description?" he asked.

"I'd know one of them if I saw him again. The moon was full and especially bright. Not a cloud in the sky." She put up her large hands to describe it better. "One was very tall and broad. He had dark hair. He turned around and was facing my way for a long moment, telling the shorter boy to hurry. His face . . . I saw clearly when he turned around. The other boy had light hair, but he never turned my way."

"What time is it?" Aunt Betty asked, confused.

"It's eight o'clock," the policeman answered.

Only eight. Ninety short minutes had passed. How slowly they had left her life, each magnified by the terror two boys had brought into her home.

Everyone around her was busy. The doctor's gentle fingers were still checking her. The policeman handed Mrs. Majinski a notebook. "It's to list possible items stolen," he explained. "Maybe someone close to her could fill it out."

"I'll give it to her niece, Candy," Mrs. Majinski said.

Candy. "Get Candy," she begged the doctor. She

didn't think he heard. Her voice was so weak, it didn't sound like her own.

Betty watched as strange hands rummaged about her bureau cabinets. The beautiful music box lay shattered on the living-room floor. In the family for as long as she could remember, and had stood for years on the end table playing softly upon command.

The silverware that had been her great-grandmother's, then passed on from grandmother to herself, gone from that box that lay empty. Warm tears flowed down Aunt Betty's cheeks. She knew she should be grateful to be alive, yet all she felt now was grief, as if someone close to her had died. All her treasures, colored scarves, lamps, pictures torn from the walls, now tossed aside as if they didn't matter. As if she didn't matter either.

She was aware of sharp pains through her body. Her legs hurt. Her back felt stiff. There was a strange pain searing across her chest and down one arm.

She was about to tell the doctor this when the stretcher was brought forward and placed next to the chair. She also wanted to tell the doctor she didn't need to be carried out, that Candy might come in and get frightened and think she was ill, but the room spun so quickly around her that all she could manage was to grasp his arm.

Then she gave in to the darkness.

7

The tears ran down Linda's cheeks as she lay looking up at her bedroom ceiling. How many times had she counted the flowers, 225 altogether, on the wallpaper extending around her room? She had counted them while she pictured how beautiful and perfect she would look someday. She had counted them as she thought of the witty things she would say and the laughter that would ripple from her throat as she entertained the crowd of friends around her. She had counted the flowers over and over, lying there quietly while her nose healed.

Only, now there was no new nose to dream of. She had it. It was smack right there in the middle of her face, all new, paid for, just as pretty as could be.

But nothing had really changed. She still felt insecure and unnoticed. No one had warned her that the inside didn't necessarily change automatically with the outside. She felt as if she had been tricked by years of expectation.

The following morning Linda ate breakfast with the despair of having faced the truth. Her mother sat across from her sipping a cup of coffee. They knew each other's thoughts only too well. Now words hung heavy between them.

"I haven't seen Candy around much lately."

"She's been busy."

"But she usually drops in after school. Are you two having a spat?"

It was the understatement of the year. A world war was more like it. But she didn't feel like getting into it with her mother. It meant unraveling the entire tale, from beginning to end, and Linda wasn't quite sure just where it had begun, nor when it would end.

She knew where it was now. Candy off on some crusade, looking like a fool in one costume after the other, everyone talking behind her back . . . in trouble with the teachers, even visiting with the school psychologist once a week because of her behavior.

"I thought once you had the operation, you would be happy," her mother persisted. "But it's evident you're not. In fact, we realize you're even unhappier than you were before."

It was obvious her parents had been discussing the matter. Linda couldn't deny their conclusion. They were right.

Linda passed up a second doughnut and further discussion of her "problem" and ran by the steps next door, glancing quickly toward the windows. Maybe she would see Candy's familiar dark eyes peering out. Perhaps if she hung around a bit more and even sat on the stoop, Candy would come out. It could be an accidental meeting. Then they might just walk to school together and their differences would dissolve.

But then Linda remembered Candy's harsh words about Pete. He was her life raft now. She couldn't risk Candy's sinking it.

She was tired of Candy's daily news bulletins regarding Pete's skirmishes. There were many things Candy didn't know about him. His father was a truck driver and was away for long periods of time. His parents didn't have much money. Pete's mother worked the night shift in the diner. He was left on his own a lot.

Linda constantly asked him over to her house. He always refused and met her in school or on the way.

"You're not going out with him at night," her mother had warned, her father joining in on that decision. "We meet him first. Then you can go. What kind of boy could he be to be unwilling to meet your parents?"

What kind of boy he could be preoccupied her thoughts the rest of the way to school. Actually she didn't know. They rarely talked, and when they did, it was usually about his motorcycle or sports. Their time together was fleeting. Pete was always on the run from some invisible threat.

"My parents won't let me go out with you until they meet you," she had told him honestly last night when he telephoned.

Her mother had hovered nearby as if reminding her of the family decision.

"They don't have to know everything you do," he answered. She kept his reply to herself.

Until now, her parents had known where she was and who she was with. But until now, Candy had been her best friend. There had been the fantasy of her new nose. Many things were changing in her life, none of them what she had expected. Perhaps what she told her parents might change also.

Empty. All the way to school, she felt emptier than the Linda sitting in the photograph on her locker door. Emptier than the one who stared at the lump in the mirror for hours. She also felt weak, because she needed Candy, because she was tempted to give in and Candy never did.

The day that had begun to unravel at breakfast fell apart during gym. A basketball bounced off the backboard and, after hitting the floor, boomeranged off the walls. As if it had aimed deliberately, the ball ended up smacking Linda squarely on the nose. As the basketball had been bouncing around quite a bit on its own before it found its target, much of its punch was lost.

But Linda, never realizing before that something might come along and endanger her priceless possession, screamed and ran to the locker room. Her entire body was quivering like a leaf caught in a windstorm. She hurried to a mirror, and until she saw there wasn't a mark, that the nose, smooth and unshaken, remained undamaged, she knew a fear unlike anything she had ever known before. It was as if she were having a nightmare and could only hope to awaken to end the horror. She bumped into Candy on her way back to her locker.

"You wouldn't be avoiding me, would you, Linda?" The hurt was fresh in the eyes facing her.

The bruise to Linda's nose had wiped away any humor she might have felt facing a rabbit with large bunny ears and a cottontail.

"Maybe I just don't need to hang around rabbits," she answered crossly.

Linda took her pocket mirror out of her purse and reexamined her nose. She felt a slight throb under the skin and a small red welt was becoming visible. She doubted its ability to withstand physical punishment and wondered how she could protect it from basketballs, baseballs, elbows. The mental list grew. She forgot all about Candy.

But Candy didn't allow that for long. Her fury fell on Linda like a clap of thunder. The rabbit ears shook and a finger pointed in Linda's direction. Candy looked like a rabbit caught in a vegetable patch.

"Well, to tell you the truth, you're no great bargain either. . . . I am so sick and tired of you and your nose. Just sick and tired of you talking about it, moping about it, as if it were the only thing in the world to worry about. I find it one great big bore." She took a deep breath as if she were about to blow Linda away. "You might not like me, Linda, but truthfully I don't even think you like yourself."

It was just what Linda needed, a reason to get it all off her chest. "And what about you, Miss Hotshot? Standing there dressed like a rabbit. Thinking you know what's best for this whole school. Who put you in charge of things?"

The rabbit took on an ominous pose, both hands on her hips. "At least I have a purpose for all of us."

"Purpose," Linda shouted back, not letting Candy finish. "Thinking you know more than anyone else around here." Before she knew it, her fingers had reached out and pulled one of Candy's floppy rabbit's ears. The makeshift ear came off in her hand. She hadn't meant to rip it. But an apology was not in order.

Candy grabbed her ear back. "You're just lucky your nose doesn't come off as easily."

"Some friend you are." Linda drew away, not trusting Candy's fist, which was curled tightly by her side.

"Me?" The rabbit now took one floppy paw and pointed to herself. "Aunt Betty was robbed last night and terrified into a heart attack. Where were you when I needed you?"

Before Linda could react to the shocking news, a small group of girls gathered nearby. Their taunting remarks were directed toward Candy.

"Hey, Candy. You like carrots?" one asked. There was a tinge of arrogance to the question.

"I bet she has a whole garden to herself," another volunteered.

The group slowly moved their way. One of the taller girls from the circle now surrounding Candy gave the orders as the others followed her instructions.

"Come on, Peter Rabbit. It's time you had a cool shower to refresh yourself. Even rabbits must get terribly mussy after gym."

Linda watched, unprepared for what happened next. The girls had circled Candy and were lifting her up so that one group held her feet while the others lifted her around the shoulders.

"Hey, let me go." Candy struggled, but she was no match for the older and bigger girls who had planned her entrance into the shower.

"Bring back the dress guide, little rabbit. What kind of a naughty rabbit are you anyway?"

Candy was well off the ground, midway in air, still clutching her dislodged rabbit's ear. "You'll ruin my outfit," she pleaded, looking frantically toward Linda as if she expected some help from that direction.

"Even rabbits dry," someone assured her from the group.

Another voice chimed in, "We're happy just the way we are. You tell all the other little rabbits to keep their dress guide in rabbit land."

Candy's body looked like a long stretcher being carried out of sight. Linda stood there, her hands turning cold, as if she were caught outside in a snowstorm without mittens. She longed to run away from the locker room, but her feet wouldn't move. Every moment of their long friendship was pulling her toward Candy, aching to give her friend support. She felt Candy's humiliation, ears flopping, feet kicking this way and that.

But then she remembered the insults spoken only a few moments before. Why would she want to defend a rabbit anyway? Especially one who hated Linda's nose and thought her a bore. It was the "bore" that hurt the most. Had Candy thought her such a nuisance all these years?

Linda put her gym suit back in the locker, the sound of screeches coming from the shower room. She heard the water turn on, laughter from the girls, then an eerie silence as everyone scattered.

There wasn't a sound from the shower. Linda waited. Then she saw Candy, water sloshing about her feet. The costume, unprepared for a drenching, stretched until the long legs were now folds about her body. An ear hung awkwardly over one eye. The makeup had run into a river of color. It was the saddest rabbit Linda had ever seen. She wanted to run to her friend and comfort her, but too much had been said between them to erase it so quickly. Instead, she hurried away, feeling the wet stare behind her.

But try as she might, she could not forget Candy's accusation. "Where were you when I needed you?" It saddened Linda to think of Aunt Betty in danger. Though she had not visited her lately, still she felt close to the woman because of the many times in the past years she had gone with Candy to visit.

She remembered her appointment with the surgeon at the last moment and rushed toward the bus stop. Linda was relieved. He could check over the healing process and she could ask him about the red welt. Then she wouldn't have to think about it anymore. Until something else happened, and it might. There was gym every day, volleyball, swimming, a hundred ways to be pushed or punched or shoved. She stood there, for the first time, wondering if

Candy was right. Was that all she ever thought about?

"How come you're at a different bus stop today?" Pete asked, on foot for a change.

"I have a doctor's appointment," she explained.

He seemed unusually bright today, almost excited. It contrasted with her glum mood nicely.

"Why the long face?" he asked.

Linda wanted to share the news with someone. Since a longer discussion with Candy was impossible, it was Pete she chose.

"Linda's Aunt Betty was robbed last night."

"Oh. Did they catch anyone?"

She was encouraged by his interest. "I don't know. Candy didn't tell me much about it. We're not exactly on the best of terms. But her aunt had a heart attack because of it."

"Well, maybe I can change your mood." He reached into the pocket of his jacket and pulled out a gold chain, then picked up her hand and dropped the piece of jewelry in it.

"For me?" she asked, surprised.

"A present. Not bad, huh?" He waited for her approval.

Linda unclasped the chain and held it up. It was a beautiful piece of jewelry. Eagerly she drew it about her neck and closed the clasp.

"Thanks, Pete." She leaned forward to kiss him lightly, but without warning, he drew her to him as if she now belonged there and the kiss was much different than she expected. It was as if, with the chain, had come the seal of ownership.

93

"Get away tonight," he ordered, holding her arm tightly, as if it was decided already.

"But my parents—"

He cut her off. "Tell them you'll be at a friend's house."

The look was sullen as the arm about her waist squeezed tightly, almost taking her breath away.

Her first instinct was to withdraw the chain from her neck and with that any claims he felt he had. But the look on his face frightened her. She didn't want to antagonize him. But she knew he was expecting something from her in return. With Pete, she now understood, you give something, you get something. He walked away as if the matter was settled.

Linda knew she desperately needed a way out of this situation, and quickly. Were Candy and she the way they used to be, Candy would have given her the support she needed to make the break.

No one just walked away from Pete Fields, not unless he wanted to let them go.

"Candy," she said aloud, "why aren't you here when I need you?"

8

"Betty, we're going to have to face facts."

Candy's mother spoke as if she had just come to an important decision. "You're just going to have to move out of that house. It isn't safe anymore. You don't need a large place like that anyway. It's too big for one person."

Aunt Betty was sitting upright, two white pillows puffed up behind her back. For the first time during the past three weeks since she had been in the hospital, there was color in her cheeks and her eyes had regained their brightness. Candy saw her aunt's shoulder stiffen, a dangerous sign from anyone in their family. A line of determination crossed her mouth. Candy was aware of her aunt's reaction to the suggestion, but her mother was too busy getting her point across to notice the change of expression from the bed.

"I've visited the nursing home several times," she went on gently but persistently, "and it's a lovely place to live. There are good doctors and nurses there, and it's safe. Not like the neighborhood you're in. Why, they haven't even caught the thieves who did this to you and it's been three weeks."

"Young lady, that house was never too big for me all these years and it's not too big for me now." The voice was strong, certain, as Aunt Betty leaned forward. "I have no intention of moving. I appreciate your concern, but you see, it's my life, my house, and my decision." The statement used up Aunt Betty's reserve of strength. She rested back on the pillows.

Candy didn't want to upset her aunt. She tried to change the subject. "When do you think you'll be leaving here?"

"In a couple of days." Aunt Betty's fingers curled about the sheets nervously. Candy suspected more was on her mind than she was willing to admit.

"Well, you definitely must come to our house to recuperate. And I'm going to the real-estate office tomorrow," Mrs. Miller stated emphatically. "We can at least find out what the house would sell for."

Candy felt she was watching a tennis game, the ball flying from one end of the court to the other. She felt miserable. Why did her aunt have to be punished because someone broke into her home? Why did Aunt Betty have to be sent away because her neighborhood was unsafe? Why couldn't the neighborhood be made safe instead? She wondered how her father would have handled it if he were here.

"Don't you worry," Mrs. Miller said, clutching Aunt Betty's hand with renewed authority. "I'll take care of everything for you. You'll see how much better off you'll be."

The final arrangements of a possible move from her home ignited Aunt Betty. She rose from the pillows like some proud lioness protecting her den. The voice was soft but controlled.

"No one, but no one," Aunt Betty repeated, and there was a tone of finality that silenced all further arguments, "is going to force me out of my family home. Not fear. Not vandalism. Not you. I will move when I want to, when I am ready to, and I am not ready now, nor do I anticipate being ready in the near future. Furthermore," her aunt's voice was now surprisingly threatening for one still recuperating, "I am quite capable of planning my own future. I have no intention of going in a direction that I am certain is wrong for me. One word right for others, but still not right for me."

The words landed like a hose full of water on a threatening fire. Nothing but the smoke was left. Candy's mother sank back in her chair, momentarily defeated. They both knew that when Aunt Betty's back went up, the issue was settled.

"I think we'd better go now." Mrs. Miller kissed Betty on the forehead. Candy went over to the side of the bed. Her aunt took both her hands in her own and squeezed them. A look of understanding passed from one to the other.

Her mother dropped Candy off at home. "I'm going to go food shopping. Want to come along?"

"Flip's coming over. We're going bike riding."

Her mother was not good at keeping things locked inside her. Candy felt there was more than Aunt Betty on her mind this morning.

97

"I haven't seen Linda around much lately."

"She's been busy." The answer was short, insufficient. It did not satisfy her mother.

"Candy, sometimes being a friend is being there when there almost doesn't seem to be a reason. I remember the nights Linda sat listening to you." The voice drifted off as painful memories returned.

Candy wondered just how long she was expected to pay back that debt. Friendship should not have to be just owing someone.

They sat there for a moment in silence, each reliving the days and months that followed the funeral, the emptying out of his closet, the visiting of close friends, then the living again.

It was obvious her mother was not succeeding on any issue this afternoon. She tried for another. "Please be careful today. Try to ride where there are people."

Candy kissed her mother. "It's O.K.," she assured her. "I'll be careful."

Flip and she picked the bicycle trail that circled the neighborhood and ran around the river. The ten-mile path that bordered the avenue and ran through the park had winding roads and a river that ran the course of the park. It was everyone's favorite, for fishing in the spring, for hikes and picnics in the summer, and for joggers and bicyclers in the winter. Though lately, even here, there was an incident now and then that led her mother to worry each time she saw the bicycles ready and waiting.

Candy looked over her shoulder and smiled. Flip's long legs pedaled furiously to keep up with her. He had on a green snowcap, but the brown curly hair managed to escape around his forehead.

Candy turned back to the street, keeping watch on the traffic and the curve of the roads. There were potholes to avoid, aside from other bicycles. Flip was now catching up, his body hunched over as if he were competing in a race. She knew he wouldn't let her lead for long. It was part of his style to know he was out in front.

Candy's attention was drawn to the ducks gliding by on the river bordering the trail. Joggers in brightly colored suits alternated with strollers. Wooden picnic tables and benches scattered about the grounds. A dozen boat houses lined the river and, at night, would light up the drive.

"I think I'm getting hungry." Flip signaled to follow him.

Candy had packed a picnic lunch. Although the air held a late-March chill, they planned to eat their sandwiches on one of the picnic tables lining the river. She followed Flip off the main road and up a small winding trail. Though the day was crystal clear and made to order for bicycle hikes, Candy's thoughts stubbornly returned to Aunt Betty. She and her aunt were not only very much alike, but in a way, they were fighting the same battle—against a small group of people going the wrong way. Perhaps they were both just individuals unafraid to stand alone.

"Aren't your legs tired?" Candy called, her cheeks bright red. She saw he was pushing a little slower and guessed the ten miles had worn him out. It was not like him to admit it.

"Let's stop here." Flip pulled over to the area where picnic tables rested under large willow trees. The sun was warm in the early afternoon, warm enough to unzipper their jackets as they spread the picnic lunch across the table.

There were peanut-butter-and-jelly sandwiches and a thermos of lemonade. Flip put on the radio and it helped fill the silence, though one of the comforting parts of their relationship was that she never felt it was necessary to fill up the spaces with talk.

"Have you been mixing any records lately?" she asked, her mouth crunching the potato chips. His lips looked extra tempting. Her attention drifted from the lemonade to the way he was chewing his sandwich.

"Now and then. Whenever I can get a job."

She decided he was very attractive and wondered how she could have thought otherwise. Candy had to admit he was being very patient when it came to their time together. If they both weren't involved with Aunt Betty's house, it was the excitement in school as the dress code conflict mounted. It was not easy for them to be alone without interruption. And then came the robbery.

With no one else at home, it was Flip Candy had called when Aunt Betty's phone kept ringing with no one at the other end to pick it up. A sense of dread engulfed her for at seven o'clock Aunt Betty was always home, always there to pick it up quickly on the second ring.

It kept ringing and ringing. Flip had driven her to the house with the green shutters. Three police cars were parked in front. Red lights flashed on and off with a sense of urgency. A crowd had gathered in front of the stoop. Only Flip's strong hand on her arm, guiding her up the steps, had given her the courage to go in.

Candy ate slowly. Flip finished long before her. He tapped his fingers on the picnic table, keeping time to the music. At last the wax paper was thrown into a garbage bucket near by, along with the paper cups.

"These benches are awfully hard," he said, shifting back and forth, waiting for her to agree. He moved from his bench to her. They watched the ducks glide by on the river. Though they were barely touching, the moment was so intense, she felt as if his arms were about her.

His arms, which she had considered too thin, were more than adequate as they finally circled her shoulders. The hard wooden benches intruded.

Flip took Candy's hand and led her the distance to the willow closer to the ducks, but away from the picnic area. There was nowhere to sit but on the ground. Flip went down first, holding her hand tightly, bringing her with him. She fell to the ground awkwardly. The two tumbled over and over, rolling on the ground, laughing, hugging, the sun following their movements.

Candy relaxed and her body leaned against him slightly as they sat together, knees propped, able to keep an eye on the picnic table and their bicycles.

They stayed that way for quite a while, the radio playing between them.

Once in a while he would look her way, and she would look his. The look would be long, certainly longer than any she would have dared to give before, and a rush of emotion would sweep through her body as if his eyes were saying all kinds of things, just for her, to be understood only by her.

It was a large willow. The limbs hung over so that they were almost invisible to anyone walking by. Slowly Flip edged his way down on to the grass until he was lying flat on his back. Candy joined him.

Flip turned over, holding a small broken-off piece of willow. He brushed the twig against her chin. His lips were fully turned up in a smile. And they were closer. Much closer.

In fact, she decided, just the right distance. She pulled his head down gently while he cooperated by moving toward her. It was a long kiss, and it awakened an appetite she never realized she possessed. Kisses before this one dulled in memory.

He sat back against the tree. She lay back, her head cushioned in his lap, the warmth of the afternoon sun almost lulling her to sleep.

The sudden change in his expression brought her fully awake. His eyes had opened wide, startled, as his entire body tensed. He was alreay half up to his knees, tossing her to the ground.

Candy followed his gaze to the picnic table. A group of a dozen boys were circling the table like a pack of vultures, moving together quickly. One jumped on Candy's bicycle. Another on Flip's. One grabbed the backpack, the other the thermos.

"They're taking our things." Candy started to pull herself to her feet, but Flip yanked her down roughly on the ground until she was lying flat on her back, protected by a large branch of the willow.

"They're stealing our bikes," she said, wrestling with him, but she was no match for Flip's strong body.

"There are ten of them, two of us," he said, pressing her against the ground as every instinct of hers fought to regain what was hers.

"They can't do that," Candy's voice was getting louder, dangerously so. Her mouth opened to shout, but Flip kissed the shout away. It was more of a kiss of anger than passion as Candy twisted under him, her fists pounding on his shoulders.

When he finally let her go, the area was empty again, the picnic table wiped clean, the bicycles now but a memory. Candy was upright, her rage fully out of control.

"How could you?" she yelled with contempt, tears of frustration spilling down her cheeks. "You stood there and let them rob us."

"What was I supposed to do, take them on, the way you're taking on Stanley High? All ten of them?"

His anger now matched hers and the moment of closeness only minutes before splattered before her eyes.

They walked the ten miles home in silence.

Candy's eyes were still filled with tears as she faced Flip on her stoop.

"I thought you believed in what I was doing. But you don't either. Well, if you won't help me change things, I'm going to change them alone." Then not waiting for his answer, she slammed the door in his face.

Standing there with her back to the door she gradually realized she was not entirely alone. She still had Sergeant Miller at her side. And she knew just what he would advise.

9

The first stop the next day was to the police station. The police chief wasn't in, but Candy made an appointment to speak to him the following week. She gathered some pamphlets and printed information from his secretary. She held on to the material all the way to school. It was her life raft. She knew now how to save Aunt Betty from moving and also how to cut down on the vandalism in school.

She saw Flip at his usual office near the pole. Even though her mother felt he had done the right thing, "Thank goodness he didn't involve you in a confrontation," and "At least you weren't hurt," nevertheless Candy expected more of him. She wanted his involvement then.

She needed it now. As soon as he saw her, Flip walked away from the small group surrounding his portable radio. The music came with him. He pulled one of Candy's Mickey Mouse ears. "I thought you gave all of this up." He wiggled the ears again.

"We're going to bring this issue to a school vote. When that happens, that's when I'll stop," she said snippily, feeling like a child having a tantrum. What she really wanted to do at this moment was ask for his help, for his support would strengthen her plan. But her pride got in the way. She couldn't bear his rejection, and he might easily say no.

Flip and his music walked with her to the front entrance of the school. Today his radio grated on her nerves, each note taking him farther away from the subject that was on her mind. Even his easygoing chatter annoyed her.

"Don't you ever take anything seriously?" she asked, taking a potshot that would bring up Saturday and the bicycle she no longer owned. It was more of an attack than a question. What she really wanted to ask him was, "If you care for me, help me," but she knew first she would have to admit she needed him. That was a long bridge for her to cross.

She had needed Linda in her life for so many years, and now it seemed her days were spent trying not to need her anymore. It was painful losing a friend. She knew the further she drew Flip into her life, the more painful the leaving.

"I take only you seriously," he answered. The brown eyes narrowed as they came closer. She felt the light touch of his lips on her forehead.

What kind of person was he, to let her say anything she wished and get away with it? Was there no end to his acceptance? She decided to test it. "I expected more of you Saturday." She didn't look at him when she said it, but rather stopped at the water fountain to get a drink. The Mickey Mouse ears fell forward as she bent down. She hoped the dress-code matter would be voted on soon, for wearing costumes was becoming not only a nuisance, but also a big bore. She heard his answer through the water splashing about her mouth.

"Sometimes, Candy, I think your problem is that you expect too much from everyone." He was gone when she looked up.

She couldn't shake the words all morning. Maybe he was right. Perhaps she did expect too much from Linda and their friendship. Was she mistaken to think it could withstand honesty, her honest feelings about Pete and his dangerous influence over her? She was about to do the same with Flip . . . put a strain on their relationship by trying to reach another level, a deeper one, one more meaningful than merely the sharing of music or a bike ride through the park.

If her thoughts were filled with shadows during history class, it only intensified the negative vibrations she felt all around her. Over the past few months, the subject of a possible dress guide being adopted had grown more serious as those against it antagonized those who suddenly awakened to its merits. Hanging from the walls and in the halls were large signs, nagging reminders of what she had come to stand for. "Bring back the dress guide. Vote Yes April 12." Another taunting message written in chalk on the classroom blackboard read, "Some pigs on the farm look classier. Let's clean up our act."

Now and then, not as often as she would have liked, someone would squeeze her hand and encourage her. But the frowns outnumbered the squeezes and the chill was in the air. Candy had never minded before being isolated from the group, for she wasn't afraid to stand alone, "straight and tall like a tree," her father had encouraged her. But today she felt as if she had been put on an island without any food rations. The prospect of being rescued looked bleak.

She glanced hopefully over toward Linda in English class, but she had her head buried in a book. Linda was combing her hair with her fingers, the way she did when she was nervous or unusually worried about something. Ordinarily, under more friendly conditions, it would have been a sign for Candy to approach her friend and find out what was bothering her. They would share the problem and work it out. But now a wall had grown between them. Each day added another brick. It was getting so high that Candy doubted if either of them would ever be able to see over it, through the resentment and distrust.

Candy dragged through English. The costume felt like another body on her back. She longed for the old clothes—any clothes, at this point. There was nothing appealing about Mickey Mouse on a day-to-day basis.

She was even running out of ideas for future costumes. Tomorrow, maybe she could come to school as the Tin Man or a witch. The loudspeaker swept away the fantasies. She knew what the voice would say even before it announced it.

Down to the school psychologist, past the smiling secretary. Mr. Hill greeted her, then slowly absorbed the black leotards, red shorts, black flippers, and the

Mickey Mouse face and ears brought back from Disneyland by a distant cousin.

He handed Candy an article from the school newspaper. It explained her involvement in bringing back a dress guide to Stanley High, but it said much more. It stated that the costumes were an effort to bring attention to the declining atmosphere in the high school.

"It's not only the dress guide," Candy now read her own words. They appeared much stronger in print than when she said them. "It's the vandalism that is accepted by everyone, including the administration."

"Your statement makes us look rather foolish here at the school." Mr. Hill circled her as if she were in a cage and he had paid the entrance fee. "We've been more than understanding about this rather bizarre way you've chosen to prove your point." He handed her a white piece of paper. "An early-dismissal notice," he explained. "Go home and remove that ridiculous getup and make sure you do not show up in it again tomorrow." He added with finality, "Or any time in the future."

Candy left Mr. Hill's office realizing it was not going to get easier. With the information from the police station still tucked in her pocketbook, she felt so close to accomplishing what she dreamed could be possible. She leaned against the door outside Mr. Hill's office and wondered if she had what it took to go all the way.

Linda walked up the hall toward her as she stood there feeling more alone and defeated than she ever had in her life. For a moment the footsteps slowed, as if she were about to stop. Candy knew the words were close to the surface for both of them. But then Linda's attention focused on the black flippers on Candy's feet. She turned abruptly and walked away, leaving Candy on her island, deserted.

Candy left the school. She decided not to go home. It wasn't too pleasant there lately either. Her mother alternated between outrage, "If you wear one more costume, young lady . . ." to embarrassment, "I can't even go to a club meeting anymore without someone bringing up this matter and you . . ." to disbelief, "You can't be dressing like that again."

Even Ian, usually in good humor and able to accept anything, had approached her this morning. "My friends think you're nuts," he said bluntly. He pointed to a bruised eye. "And because I'm your brother, they think I'm nuts too." He was asking her to stop. Part of her wanted to take the Mickey Mouse costume off that very moment. But another part said, Don't let them make you give in, something better is on the other side.

Instead of walking home, she walked down the avenue, by the pizza place. Everyone waved, appreciating Mickey Mouse on the warm spring day. The barber came out and inspected her outfit. The owner of the bakery shop wiped her hands on her apron, handed Candy a doughnut, laughed, and said, "You're just what we need to attract business."

Candy knew they needed much more. They needed to be able to operate their businesses in

110

safety without the guard dogs and bars on the windows.

Then she reached Pop Williams' store, now the bowling alley, but to her, always, the location at which her father died. She stood in front of the large picture window, not seeing the bowling alleys, nor the bowlers, but rather the fruits and vegetables, hearing her father's laughter as he picked some hard candy from the cart Pop had always kept filled for the children. She stood there, her feet unable to move forward. Her father could have passed by Pop Williams' stand and not become involved. But Pop was a neighbor, and her father cared about his neighbors. He had left her that. She wouldn't betray his legacy.

Of course she would go on. He would have. Candy walked slowly to Aunt Betty's house. She carried an important gift for her. Aunt Betty was home from the hospital for over a week, refusing to stay at Candy's home. "My house has been left alone for too long." If she was frightened about returning, she hid it carefully.

In her pocketbook was a timer Aunt Betty could hang about her neck so that her pots, or the house, wouldn't burn down. "She's getting so forgetful lately," Candy's mother insisted. It was just another reason added on to all the others to remove Aunt Betty from the premises.

Aunt Betty answered the door. She was sleeping temporarily in the living room on the sofa. It was made up with a blanket and pillow.

"Oh, what a nice surprise. So many visitors today." She led Candy into the house as if she had been expecting Mickey Mouse to show up, but then again, her aunt seemed to understand Candy without words. It was that feeling between them of never having to explain that Candy treasured. Just as Aunt Betty never had to explain to her why she wore wide skirts, shawls, and white sunglasses all year round.

"Look what Flip is doing." Aunt Betty pointed to the kitchen. There was Flip installing a dead-bolt lock on the back door. There was a new window in the kitchen. "Difficult to break," Aunt Betty explained.

Candy sat down on the couch, suddenly very tired and unsure about her plans for Aunt Betty's safety. Though there was a new, more secure lock on the door, the door itself was so weak, it could easily be kicked in. They would have to substitute a stronger one. The windows were frail thoughout the house. A bright light transformed the backyard from an ominous patch of land to a blend of trees and flowers. Yet it wasn't enough.

The aroma of garlic and meat drifted from the oven. Candy realized this might be the only place she could come and feel comfortable. Certainly not home now. Nor with Linda.

"Mrs. Majinski put the roast in the oven. She'll be in later for dinner," Aunt Betty explained from the couch. "Everyone's fussing over me so."

Candy pulled the leather flippers off her feet. She removed the ears and mask like a soldier shedding her uniform after battle. She stretched her long legs while Flip turned the doorknob to test it.

Aunt Betty's gentle snoring told Candy she had not yet regained all her strength. At last Flip sat down next to her, his arm around her shoulder. She worked her way deeper into the hollow of it.

"I'm sorry," she said from somewhere under his chin.

"I needed to know that," he answered honestly.

Candy knew it was now or never. If they were to be close, she had to reach out for his help.

"Wait a minute." She got up and opened her pocketbook. "Look." She spread out the pamphlets on the table in front of them. The front of one brochure held the bold words, "Neighborhood Watch." Others stated, "Mobile Townwatch—Prevent Crime."

"It's neighbors watching over one another's houses, patroling in cars when necessary. We could start it here." It was not a simple task she was suggesting. It would take time and commitment. She didn't know if he was willing to volunteer either.

Flip opened the brochures and skimmed through the pages.

"I have an appointment with the police chief next week," Candy added. "If we could get it started, there could be people driving around here in cars without weapons, but with a CB radio, able to call into the police on anything suspicious." Candy didn't feel it necessary to tell him that a school watch might also be appropriate, students watching over one another's lockers. That could come later.

Flip was concentrating on the pile of reading

material before him. Candy looked over at her aunt. She lay there, so fragile, graceful, but so vulnerable and trusting. It had to work.

"Look at this." Flip shared the page with her. "'The police department offers free services. They'll inspect your house and nearby grounds. A detective sergeant will suggest improvements in security for your home and grounds. Engraving tools can be lent to the community to mark bicycles, tools, lawn mowers, rings, even appliances so that positive identification can be made should they be stolen.'"

"You see," Candy pointed out, "if there was a neighborhood watch program in this neighborhood, Aunt Betty could remain in her home with a reasonable amount of safety." She hoped her enthusiasm would be contagious. "Neighbors driving by in a car would notice a broken window, a darkened house, someone suspicious running through the yard.

"It'll take plenty of work to organize block captains, coordinators. Maybe even a newsletter." She wished he would say something. Was he waiting for her to ask?

"I need your help," she said at last. It was not just asking for his aid today, but for tomorrow, and perhaps weeks past that.

"Sure," he said, so easily it was almost like an embrace. They sealed the new project with a real hug.

Later that evening Candy found it difficult to get to sleep. The possibilities of the neighborhood watch program overwhelmed her. She closed her eyes, now so overtired she wondered if sleep would ever come. At first, because it had been so long since she had heard it, she thought it was just the creaking of the house in the cold night. Candy sat up in bed, listening for it again. One, two, three, four, five, six knocks against the wall. It was their signal to meet outside on the stoop. Quickly Candy wrapped the heavy blanket about her, slipped into her bedroom slippers, and hurried quietly down the steps.

Linda sat there on the stoop, wrapped in a blanket, waiting. Candy sat down beside her, wondering which of them would speak first. Because she couldn't decide, she looked up at the sky. Every star that was available shone brightly.

"I don't think there should be any restrictions on dress," Linda began, as if it was necessary to establish sides.

"You're entitled to your opinion." Candy wrapped the blanket tightly around her. She didn't appreciate being called out in the middle of the night for another argument. Yet she knew instinctively that if she left this time, there would be no coming back.

Many minutes passed by with nothing said. It was an uncomfortable silence, unlike the kind she and Flip shared. The wall, which had taken so many weeks to build, was now standing tall and strong between them.

"I guess I haven't been much of a friend lately." The statement came from Linda, but Candy knew it could have come from herself as well.

"Me neither," she answered. They finally agreed on something. Then, because it was the truth, because one of them had to strike a hard blow at the wall to knock it down, Candy continued, "I really need you as my friend, Linda. There aren't that many people around I can depend on." She was thinking of the dependable people—her mother, Flip, Aunt Betty, and of course, Linda. The circle was small.

Linda responded with warmth. Even in the dark Candy could see the smile. "That's just what I was going to say. There aren't that many people who will accept me just the way I am." She paused. "Pop-up toasters and all . . . you know what I mean."

"And the shoes by the bed." Candy held her hand over her mouth, but the laughter slipped out.

"What about the tom-toms?" Now it was Linda holding her sides.

As usual, as it happened since they were little girls, the smiles turned to uncontrollable laughter. They shushed each other, but the night was too soft and still, their giggling too eager. Unfortunately the noise traveled to the upstairs bedrooms.

The overhanging door lights clicked on, first over one door, then the other.

"Candy," her mother whispered from the front-bedroom window, the breeze sending the command straight to its destination. "Get up here before you catch pneumonia."

"Linda, what do you think you're doing out there?" The window next door opened wide. Mrs. Tucker stuck her head out and waved to Mrs. Miller.

The two girls pulled the blankets up about their ankles as they approached the doorways.

"Just to show you Pete isn't all bad, look what he

bought me." Linda opened the blanket and pointed to her neck.

Candy knew she would have to accept Pete if she were to maintain Linda's friendship. She fingered the chain. It shone brightly underneath the light. "It's beautiful," she said.

"Girls!" the voice from the upstairs window ended the conversation as the two scurried up the steps. Candy ran past her mother, who stood in her nightgown waiting to lock the door and close the house down for good.

Just as she was dozing off, Candy heard the three taps on the wall. She smiled sleepily, then raised her hand over the bed and tapped back. Everything was moving back into place again.

Then suddenly she bolted upright in bed, her eyes wide with shock. She remembered she had seen that same gold chain with the ten round links that Linda was wearing. It was exactly like the one stolen from Aunt Betty.

10

Candy picked out her clothes quickly this morning, listening for the knock on the wall that would tell her Linda was ready.

The past week had been tense but rewarding since Candy had discovered Aunt Betty's chain around Linda's neck. She had told Linda her suspicions and was surprised to find relief on her face, as if the necklace had not really been a gift she wanted to keep. Linda anxiously confided her doubts about Pete and the two together went to the police station.

Aunt Betty identified the chain as the very one her old boyfriend had given her. "Exactly ten round links amid all the square ones," she stated as if there could be no doubt.

From there, the police set the date for the preliminary hearing . . . which would be held tomorrow. Mrs. Majinski would finally have the opportunity to identify Pete Fields as one of the two who had fled from Aunt Betty's house across the backyard.

Linda had taken it all much better than Candy expected, cooperating with the police, giving them the details as to exactly when Pete had given her the gift.

Candy only wished her mother were as cooperative on her other plans. "A neighborhood watch program?" She had looked at Candy doubtfully at breakfast. "If Aunt Betty weren't so stubborn, she would listen to me and sell the house and that would be that."

For today, the three of them, Flip included, were to go to the police station to get the details on organizing the neighborhood watch. Linda had asked to be included. It was like old times again, except the friendship seemed richer for the growing it had done.

The radio blared loudly all the way to the police station. The Township Building was a one-story brick complex that looked more like it housed business offices than the police. An American flag hung in the hallway.

They waited in an outer office. A secretary took them into Police Chief Kellman's meeting room. He looked impressive in his uniform, sitting behind the large desk.

"It's going to take a lot of work on the part of all of you to get this thing off the ground." He sat back surveying them as if he were measuring their sincerity. "You're going to have to knock on plenty of doors to get block captains and volunteers." He waited, as if expecting a pledge or sign of commitment. Or perhaps a hint that one of them would back down.

"My aunt lives on South Nineteenth Street in that

neighborhood. She lives alone, but she isn't safe living there the way things are," Candy offered. And then, because she felt it was important to say and because she was proud to say it, she added, "I'm Sergeant Joe Miller's daughter.

She hadn't had an opportunity to say it quite like that before, and realized she wanted to do just that for the past three years. She wondered if her mother ached to let it out as well. Maybe she would help her try.

"You lost your father. We lost a fine policeman that day." Chief Kellman cleared his throat and shuffled the papers in front of him. "We'd like to make it safer, Candy, on your aunt's block and everyone else's, but there are just so many policemen available and just so much money to hire them. We can't possibly keep an eye on all of the houses." He sounded as if he wished he could.

Chief Kellman had broad shoulders, like a football player's. His eyes were blue, very clear, and when he talked, they had a way of looking straight at whomever he was speaking to. He outlined the plan that would start the neighborhood watch program in Aunt Betty's vicinity. "First you have to get the people interested. Most, at first, just won't care. They have their own problems. The little time this would take might be too much for them. Others just might not care to get involved."

Candy looked to Flip for support. She took hold of his hand while the chief gave them the bleak facts.

Linda persisted past the obstacles. "If we get at

least one volunteer captain per block, will that be enough?"

"That should be fine," the chief continued. "Everyone on the street will have the block captain's phone number to report anything to. People do not have to give their names when they report their information. Many are afraid of retribution. So many citizens don't come forward with the facts because they are afraid that those who robbed them will punish them for coming to the police."

"Is that true?" Flip asked.

They were both thinking of Mrs. Majinski, her frightened eyes when asked to be a witness.

"Very seldom. Those who rob houses don't necessarily feel like hanging around. They come, get what they want out, get out. Barking dogs, lights, quality locks, make them uneasy and often discourage them."

They listened attentively while Chief Kellman outlined their campaign. It was as if Aunt Betty's neighborhood was a war zone and the three of them were to bring in the troops. At last, Candy realized, they were fighting back.

"The block captain reports his calls to the police. This helps us decide what calls are urgent and enables us to answer the calls quickly. For instance," Kellman continued, "in one neighborhood, a woman spotted a car outside her home. It was parked for quite a long time. Someone was sitting in the car. The woman was alone, her husband out of town. She called the block captain. The captain called the police. The police, who had their hands full with a five-car accident on the expressway that night, notified the mobile townwatch. While all this was going on, the block captain was on the telephone with the woman, calming her, giving her a feeling that she wasn't alone and that her problem was being taken care of."

"What happened to the car?" Flip asked, as if he were following the threads of a mystery story.

"The townwatch sent out neighbors involved in the program who parked a distance away, but not too far from the automobile in question. The volunteers watched to see if anyone departed or entered, and used their CB radio to report back to the police station. After about a half-hour, a girl came out of a house nearby, got into the car, and the driver drove off. But the townwatch had the license number. Now the police were aware of the car. If it ever showed up again under suspicious circumstances, it would be checked again. By the way, our mobile townwatch does not carry weapons."

"It seems to work," Linda said enthusiastically.

"It does, and very well. It's neighbors watching over one another."

The chief handed Flip and Candy some bright red emblems. They read, "Member—Operation Lookout—Neighborhood Watch. A program in our township where residents look out for their neighbors' homes."

"You can give those out as you go around." Chief Kellman handed each of them some yellow decals which stated, "Member National Sheriff's Association—Neighborhood Watch Program-warning . . . Prevent Burglaries."

"Well, I guess that's it," Flip said, looking ready to leave. He had used up his small supply of patience.

"Wait. Before you go, let me read this to you." The police chief opened up a small brochure. "Feel free to ask any question as I go along. 'The Neighborhood Watch Program is a self-help crime-prevention program to reduce threats to you and your neighbors' property. It is an active participation in a law-enforcement and citizen cooperative battle against crime, its primary purpose being the protection of your own and your neighbors' property.' You should memorize this section," the chief advised, "so that you will be able to convey its message to the neighbors as you get to meet them. You'll have to explain just where all of you fit into the program and why you believe it should be started. You're going to have to sell the idea."

It was Flip who was now assuring the police chief that they intended to see it through until the program was on its way.

"Is that it?" Flip asked, the folders under his arm as he stood ready to go, his eagerness getting the best of him.

The police chief rose and shook hands with them. "It's up to you now," he said, "and everyone else in Aunt Betty's neighborhood."

Linda and Flip carried on the conversation during the drive to Aunt Betty's house. Candy barely heard them. She had begun to read the pamphlet the police chief had given her. Suddenly she was made aware of the information on the pages. She was just as guilty of being careless about crime prevention as everyone else. The do's and don't's of the booklet reminded her of the front door of her home, which was usually unlocked and wide open in the springtime. The pamphlet instructed her to keep it locked and always to ask who was on the other side of the door before opening it. She promised herself to remember and to tell her mother what she was learning about the safety of their family. There were also thick bushes around her house and in front of the living-room windows. She realized as she read on that the bushes could easily conceal someone who wished to break into the front window. The pamphlet suggested they be trimmed and that there be adequate lighting in the front and back of all houses.

Flip pulled up in front of Aunt Betty's house. They had decided to include her in their neighborhood watch plans, hoping that it would increase her own peace of mind while recuperating. The three of them walked around the back of the house, through the backyard. Candy had a key to the back door. Before she had a chance to unlock it, the door opened to her touch.

"I don't believe it," Candy said, stunned. "She's left it opened. Anyone could walk inside."

They were standing in the kitchen, looking at one another in disbelief.

"Is that you, Mrs. Majinski?" the voice called from the living room.

"It's us, Aunt Betty," Candy answered. "We'll be right there."

Linda came forth as the realist in the group. "If locks are the first line of defense in a robbery, at least that's what my booklet says, well, a deadbolt lock is not effective if it's unused."

They passed around the cookie jar. It had the same face as the one destroyed in the robbery. "I bought several at one time," Aunt Betty had explained when she set the new one on the table last week.

"We're going to have to talk to your aunt," Flip said firmly. "Nothing we do will do any good if we don't have her cooperation."

Aunt Betty sat on her favorite spot on the couch. There was more color to her cheeks and her eyes held a brightness that Candy had worried she might never see again.

"My goodness, you three look so serious today. Go take some cookies. You'll feel better."

That was usually her prescription for any down day in Candy's life. Most of the time it worked. Today it didn't. The box of pick-up sticks was on the table. Candy guessed she was practicing. She decided now was not the time to pursue the unlocked doors. Perhaps later, alone, she might leave the brochures, and hopefully Aunt Betty would understand herself that old habits would have to be changed.

It was Linda who sat down on the couch next to Candy's aunt. "I'm so sorry," she apologized. "When I found out it was Pete," her voice broke.

"Nonsense, child." Aunt Betty pulled her protectively in a hug. "I'm just glad you're out of reach of that dangerous boy."

The doorbell rang and Aunt Betty jumped up with all her old energy. "I'll get it," she said.

Candy noticed she opened the door without even asking who was on the other side. There was no wide-angle spy hole to identify visitors as the police chief had suggested.

"Never admit anyone unless you know them," the police had cautioned. How easily her aunt whisked open her front door at the first knock without even asking, "Who's there?" It was as if everyone on the other side were a friend. She wondered how many people felt the same way. Though Aunt Betty's robbery had left her physically shaken, as the weeks drifted by she obviously had fallen back into her old habits of trust.

Mrs. Majinski's voice filled the hallway. She was standing there, hands twisting in her apron, eyes streaming with tears.

"I can't do it. I just can't do it," the voice was quivering, frightened, unlike the strong, certain voice Candy was accustomed to.

"I'm afraid if I testify, they'll come after me. You know they could, and it's just Mr. Majinski and me alone now. The children are all gone," the voice went on pleading for understanding from the group around her.

"Did something happen, Mrs. Majinski?" Flip asked.

"A telephone call . . . it was a terrible voice . . . this morning . . . threatening . . ." She broke off, wiping her forehead with the edge of her apron.

Aunt Betty settled the matter with a cup of hot tea. They all sat around the kitchen table now, silently looked into their teacups as if the answers might be found at the bottom.

It was Flip who first offered hope of a solution. "Mrs. Majinski, if you didn't have to testify alone, if we could have some strong-looking people around you, and a lot of them, would you reconsider?"

Mrs. Majinski thought for a moment, her wide eyes now less fearful. "Yes, I would feel better, but who would come? Who would even care? In this neighborhood, no one does."

That's what the three of them spent the rest of the night finding out. Who would care?

Candy and Linda took one side of the street, Flip the other. They knocked on each door, showing the decals, explaining the material. Throughout all of it, they told and retold the story of Aunt Betty's robbery and Mrs. Majinski's need for support. They asked for volunteers to come down to the preliminary hearing so that Pete Fields would understand that Mrs. Majinski and Aunt Betty did not stand alone, but were part of a larger group that would protect and defend them at any cost.

Some people shut the door in their faces. Others shook their heads and said they'd think about it. The elderly couple who were knocked down in front of the supermarket said to count them in. The man whose dog Pepper was mysteriously poisoned wanted to be included, "For Pepper also," he explained.

Later that night, the three of them sat on Aunt Betty's stoop, tired and uncertain. They had covered about thirty homes and uttered thousands of words.

Still they didn't know. The preliminary hearing was tomorrow. Only then would the question be answered. Did anyone care?

11

It was a week Candy would never forget. It began with the preliminary hearing.

"They look much younger than I would have thought," Aunt Betty murmured, holding tightly on to Candy's arm. Mrs. Majinski sat next to her, the usual color gone from her cheeks, her arm entwined through Aunt Betty's as if she didn't dare let go.

It had taken a lot of knocking on doors but the effort was not in vain: thirty neighbors showed up. They sat on benches and chairs, whispering to one another in the police station.

Though it was only a preliminary hearing, Mrs. Majinski decided to testify. "If I'm going to, I might as well start right away."

"That other boy looks like a child." Aunt Betty shook her head, dismayed at the youth who sat between his parents.

When it was her turn, Mrs. Majinski testified, pointing to Pete Fields as one of the boys she had seen run across Aunt Betty's backyard the night of the robbery. Aunt Betty identified the chain as her own, and the policeman on duty the night of the robbery gave his testimony.

What wasn't expected was a large burly man, a neighbor living two houses down from Aunt Betty, who stood up in the back of the room and spoke at the end of the hearing.

"We want those boys to know that all of us are neighbors of Betty Jenson and Mrs. Majinski. We're here today because we don't want anything to happen to these two ladies . . . or to anyone else on that block. We neighbors want to make that clear. That robbery affected all of us."

The guilty look on Pete's face told all those present that the message struck home. Pete's parents were unable to post a bond for bail. He was held at a detention center pending trial.

"It makes me feel better to know he's no longer on the street," Aunt Betty said quietly as they left.

The following morning Candy packed her costumes in a box. She left only one out, the black skunk outfit she'd been saving for just such an occasion. Today was the day chosen by the school newspaper for all those in favor of a dress guide to come to school dressed in costume. With others supporting her, Candy felt she couldn't be expelled. Yet she faced the day with uncertainty. There was no way of telling just how many would actually wear costumes to indicate support.

The tail of the skunk was like a plume, black and white. Candy slid into the outfit, smiling as she remembered Aunt Betty's comment when she gave it to her.

"I saw it in that novelty store and couldn't resist it." She had handed it to Candy boxed like a birthday present. "You seem to be enjoying wearing costumes so much these days."

Candy made up her face, slipping the mask over her eyes.

When she sat down at the breakfast table, her mother's face tightened as if there was a gusher of words locked inside.

"There's your new lock." Her mother set the lock down firmly on the kitchen table. "It finally occurred to me, it was unreasonable for me to expect the school to buy two thousand expensive locks. But we certainly can take care of just your locker."

Candy wondered if there was a hidden message in her mother's statement. Was she hinting that perhaps Candy was expecting too much from her classmates and from Stanley High School? Candy put the lock in her pocketbook with a quiet thank you, then finished her cereal.

It didn't really seem like much of a victory to her, though she didn't want to hurt her mother's feelings by telling her so. The problem of vandalism still existed.

"Now all you have to do is memorize the combination." Her mother rushed about the kitchen, trying to avoid the skunk's tail. "I wrote down the combination also. The principal had mixed feelings about my buying the lock, because he said all of the locks put on by the school are recorded by combination in the main office. That way, if they ever have to get into your locker, they have your combination on hand. But I told the principal I don't trust their records anyway. Well, they reluctantly agreed, until a better solution comes along, anyone who wishes can get their own locks and have their own combination."

Candy didn't want to diminish her mother's accomplishment, for it was an impressive one, but dealing with one locker and with each individual worrying about himself was not exactly what Candy had in mind.

"I'm not coming right home after work, so make sure you have a key."

"Are you going to Aunt Betty's?"

"No, but the matter concerns her. I have an appointment with a rental agent for one of those apartment complexes that specialize in renting to people Aunt Betty's age. I think they might have an opening for her."

It sounded better than a home, but it was still moving Aunt Betty out of the place she loved. "You can't force her," Candy said in behalf of her aunt. She felt her mother's disapproval in the mouth that tightened.

"No, we can't. I don't intend to." There was an edge of hostility in the voice. "But just how long do you think she'll be able to carry on in a neighborhood that isn't safe any longer?"

The argument was a valid one. Though the neighbors had rallied for the preliminary hearing, when she asked them to stay for the first neighborhood watch meeting, all but three gave excuses and left. She knew there would be weeks of work ahead before the entire neighborhood was involved. Could Aunt Betty wait it out and remain safe?

As if her mother read her mind, she dug into Candy's doubts. "Aunt Betty is not safe in her house and that's that. There could be another Pete Fields lurking out there, and next time she might not be so lucky." There was a long pause. "Your cooperation would help," her mother said as the doorbell rang. "You have more influence over your aunt than anyone of us. You and Flip could convince her to do what is best in the long run. You both keep encouraging her to stay, but have you considered the danger you're placing her in?"

The words stung. Perhaps they were actually endangering her aunt by helping her fix up the place. Candy shook her head stubbornly, hanging on to her last defense. "I can't do that to her. It isn't right, forcing anyone to do what you want them to do, just because it makes you feel better."

The constant ringing of the doorbell relieved them both of the necessity to go on.

Candy gathered her books, her confidence fading.

"I don't believe it," Candy heard her mother's voice rise an octave higher as she opened the door. "Not you too."

It was Linda's voice coming into the kitchen, but it was a lion with broom bristles as whiskers and an orange dust mop for hair. A sign on the lion's chest read, "I don't want anyone telling me what clothes to wear in my jungle."

"I give up." Candy's mother walked out of the room, her head shaking in disbelief.

"You didn't think there was just one side to this issue." The lion mouth opened wide, and then laughed. "May the best animal win."

The lion and the skunk walked down the stoop together, leaving Candy's mother with her hands thrown up in the air in frustration. . . .

When Linda had mentioned there would be others dressed in costume today, Candy assumed perhaps a few more would be involved. She wasn't prepared for the group waiting for her when she walked into school. It was larger than she expected with some kids roaming about the halls dressed as pussycats and pirates, rabbits and lions, and a couple of snowmen. Signs were everywhere, for and against a dress guide. Obviously the school newspaper had brought both sides out in the open.

Candy sat down in her seat in English class, savoring every moment of it. She was certain Mr. Hill would not be calling her down to his office today, not unless he also called down everyone else around her.

The battle continued all week. Queens, kings, witches, and goblins attended class, filling the halls with long skirts and magic wands. From the count of animal getups, Stanley High could have been mistaken for a zoo.

One student wore a sign over his tramp outfit. "We need guidelines for dress."

On the other hand, another, in barber outfit, wore a poster which read, "If you're old enough to enlist, you're old enough to know what to wear."

Flip showed up at school as a rock star. In his fuchsia sunglasses, flared pants and striped shirt, guitar strung over one shoulder, he could have given a concert and filled the stands. The note on his guitar read, "Nobody tells a star what to wear." Candy was surprised. He was on the other side.

In reality, though, it didn't matter whose side he was on or whose side would win. What was important was that gradually the entire school was stirring again, as if awakening from a long sleep. It was fighting back, but with humor, in fun, and some of her classmates were using their imagination to do it. Perhaps she had judged them too quickly, and too harshly.

Debates dotted the hallways. A rabbit and a lion stood by the water fountain arguing. A group of munchkins sat with the Scarecrow of Oz in the lunchroom in animated conversation.

"Well, you did it this time." Flip put his guitar down beside the lunch table and took half of Candy's sandwich. "The school board is having a meeting Wednesday night. They intend to deal with the dress-guide issue. Truthfully," he said with exaggerated confidence, "I think my side is going to win." He slipped his arm about her waist and gently squeezed it. She knew, at this point, they were all going to win. The victory was all around her, in the excitement of her classmates.

On the Wednesday of the school-board meeting, a ballot was cast. Each class voted for or against suggested guidelines for dress to be included in the school handbook. The teachers were careful to count the votes, making sure no one voted twice. All the ballots were brought to the main office, where they were sorted and counted, the results to be announced in assembly after the school-board meeting.

No one was late to school Thursday morning. A special assembly was called. The first order of business was to announce that Halloween was over at Stanley High and everyone would be expected to attend class in their regular clothes. The second order of business was to explain just what those clothes would be.

Amid shouts of "We won! We won!" the principal read the new grooming guide aloud.

"The board passed the following suggested dress and grooming guide last night," he explained.

Candy noticed his hair was newly cut. He wore a bright blue tie and a fresh white shirt under his suit.

The students finally calmed down as the guidelines were read.

1. Body cleanliness is essential.
2. Fingernails should be cleaned and neatly trimmed.
3. Boys faces should be clean shaven.
4. Hair should be clean, neat, trimmed, and combed.
5. For boys, a shirt with sleeves is appropriate. Shirt tails should be tucked in. Shirt must be worn at all times. For girls, a blouse or sweater with skirt is suggested.
6. Trousers and skirts should be clean and neatly pressed.
7. Shoes or other appropriate footwear must be

worn at all times. Shoes should be clean and polished.

8. Extreme styles or modes of dress or grooming should be avoided. In selecting wearing apparel for school, modesty and community norms of decency should be a consideration.

The principal cleared his throat, then continued. "Copies of the suggested dress and grooming guide will be distributed in your classrooms."

A roar of approval went up about the room, as Candy's supporters crowded about her. Candy sensed a new energy in the auditorium, as if they were all embarking upon a new journey together.

But the best moment of all was when her mother wrapped her in her arms that night, tears mixed with laughter as she cried, "Oh, Candy, I'm so proud of you. You're your father's daughter."

It had been many days since Candy had looked through her father's scrapbook. Later that evening she sat on the bed, flipping the pages slowly. It was almost as if one page lingered under her fingers a little longer than the rest. She read the poem on the page aloud—as if it were a message sent especially to her.

Be the Best of Whatever You Are

If you can't be a pine on the top of the hill
Be a scrub in the valley—but be
The best little scrub by the side of the rill.
Be a bush if you can't be a tree.

If you can't be a bush—be a bit of the grass,
Some highway happier make;
If you can't be a muskie, then just be a bass—
But the liveliest bass in the lake.

We can't all be captains, we've got to be crew.
There's something for all of us here,
There's big work to do, and there's lesser to do
And the task we must do is the near.

If you can't be a highway, then just be a trail,
If you can't be the sun, be a star.
It isn't by size that you win or you fail—
Be the best of whatever you are!

                                    By Douglas Malloch

Candy sat there on the bed, her eyes bright with excitement. "I promise, Dad," she said, as if he were sitting across from her, "I'll keep doing the best that I can."

She knew somehow that now meant getting the attention of all of Aunt Betty's neighbors, so that they would want to become involved in one another's lives. Candy slept with the scrapbook under her pillow, hoping she would wake up with the solution.

12

The posters for the block party had been hanging on poles all week. No one had ripped them down. That was the first clue that there had been a silent acceptance of the event by the neighbors living in the row homes between South Eighteenth Street and South Nineteenth Street. An organizational meeting of block captains two weeks before the party had formed the skeleton crew. Many families had volunteered to help. Mrs. Majinski was named neighborhood watch coordinator. She immediately took charge, assigning jobs to everyone. The block-party committee quickly grew to twenty busy people making telephone calls, scheduling meetings, seeking donations of food, equipment, tables. The two weeks passed by quickly. Flip and Candy hung fliers on every pole and space available. Now the day was here.

"What is it? the flier asked. "It's an old-fashioned block party, featuring food, games, entertainment, prizes. Beginning 12:00 Saturday, April 28. Purpose . . . the Neighborhood Watch Program is beginning in Oran County and what better way to launch it than a party? A day to get to know one another, to get to know our neighborhood and care about it. Our neighborhood will be blocked off for Saturday, and the park will be used for the big afternoon softball game.

Games and Events

Egg Toss   Sprints   All Ages

Relay Races   Dance Contest

Door Prizes   Bubble-gum Contest

Softball Game   Tug-of-war   Face-painting Contest

Bring a dessert to be placed on the free sweet table.

Bring a large size trash bag for clean up after.

Drop off objects at your block captain's home for use in a white elephant sale.

"All proceeds to help defray costs of the block party and to go into Neighborhood Watch Fund."

The streets were still empty. Candy's mother had dropped her and Linda off with two large tin tables and a stack of records.

"I'll be over later," her mother promised. She was still dubious regarding Candy's project. But she had given in on another front. Aunt Betty's stubbornness had won out. There was now to be no more mention of her moving out of her home.

Candy had her own doubts about the block party. It was possible the plan would fail, the neighbors not show up at all. She had been thinking of that possibility all week. Her first worry was rain. If it rained, there was a rain date, but still, it meant canceling and rescheduling. Looking up at the clear cloudless sky, Candy realized the weather, at least, was on their side. She only hoped the neighbors were also.

"Where do you want this table?" Linda dragged a large cardboard box to the curb and pulled the table out of it.

Candy stood in the center of the street like a traffic cop. "Put that one up there toward the end of the block." She pointed.

The white roadblocks were up already, sectioning off two blocks from traffic. Flip and she contacted the highway department for use of the barricades. At the same time they had been granted township permission to hold the party. He had informed Candy he would put an extra patrol car on duty to keep an eye on the neighborhood while everyone was enjoying the party. She saw a patrol car drive up to the barricade and park.

If everyone came to the gathering . . . if anyone came . . .

Now and then a sleepy face stared back at Candy from an upstairs window. It was only nine in the morning. Many people were just stirring on a lazy Saturday morning.

Linda stood behind a table as if it were a counter and she the salesgirl. Though there was nothing on it, she looked very professional. Candy was relieved to have her support. Though they had talked out their differences many nights now on the stoop, she knew Linda had become a different person than the one she had grown so used to. A new and exciting dimension had been added to their friendship. "I have no intention of being Candy Miller's clone," she stated flatly, without anger, but with a new assertiveness Candy could only respect.

Candy felt a surge of relief when a purple car with one white door pulled around the corner. If she had learned nothing else about Flip, it was that his car was his source of pleasure, second only to his portable radio. He changed its color almost as often as Candy changed costumes.

Linda and Candy pulled the roadblock aside and Flip's car pulled in.

"I'll keep the car parked near the end here." Flip's arms were filled with records as he backed out of the car. "The rest of the equipment is in the back seat and trunk."

They helped Flip unload the car. "I'm going to need a large table," he said. "I've brought a heavy extension cord. Now all I've got to do is find a place to plug it in. Maybe someone in one of the houses . . ." He disengaged himself and walked up the steps of the row home closest to them. Candy waited as he knocked on the door. No one answered. Flip quickly went to the adjoining house, where finally the door was opened by a sleepy-eyed man in a bathrobe. After a few minutes' conversation, Flip ran back to the car, unwound the extension cord until it reached the front steps, then slithered into the house.

"We're in business," he said proudly, returning to the car. "We've got the music. Now I can get my equipment going." The recreation department had loaned them their PA system and bullhorn.

A few more cars were pulling up to the blockade.

Candy recognized some of the block captains and their families. Many carried tables, others trash bags. The tables were opened and filled up the curbs. Brightly colored tablecloths gave the street a festive look.

A woman handed Candy a list of gifts donated from shops on the avenue for prizes. Candy was surprised at its length. She made a memo in a small notebook she carried to write thank-you notes to all the businesses involved.

The children of the families were busy covering the tables with plants and dishes, items collected for the white elephant sale.

A man walked up to Candy with a peanut cannon in his hands. He had constructed it himself and promised it would shoot peanuts into the air. He put on an immediate demonstration for Candy. She broke into laughter, the tension fading from the day as peanuts filled the air and splattered about the street. He brought his own card table and proceeded to set it up.

Aunt Betty came scurrying up the block, two boys about Flip's age in tow, both carrying bags.

"Where do you want these?" one puffed, clearly feeling the strain of Aunt Betty's collection. Candy waved them over to the corner, next to the peanut machine. She recognized the plastic bags as donations from Aunt Betty's accumulated treasures. She had managed to fill up the living room again, though she had confided to Candy, "My money now goes in the bank . . . all of it."

"We'll be at the elephant sale." Aunt Betty

straightened her hat properly. She was dressed in a long skirt, with a cape over her shoulders. Her hat brought with it the first sign of spring. It was bright blue with a yellow flower perched in front. As she fluttered about from table to table, taking charge as if it were her own private tea party, Candy hoped for her aunt's sake that the day would be a success.

The face-painting contest was now in operation. A little girl with yellow pigtails was standing patiently while circles, colors of the rainbow, gradually covered her forehead.

Signs were popping up all over the place. PICNIC AREA—GAMES AND RACES—DRINKS. Flags and balloons waved in the air.

Candy felt like a school guard standing in the center of the street, her neighborhood watch badge clinging to her jacket as she directed people to different areas of the street, handing out decals and fliers. There was a large sign posted on a curb. "THIS IS A NEIGHBORHOOD WATCH PROGRAM."

Linda ran by with little smiles painted all over her face. She was balancing cake plates overflowing with delicious-looking desserts.

Flip let her know he meant business as his music broke through the loudspeaker and drifted up the street. Candy saw a few windows pushed up and a few down. It was nearly eleven o'clock, and there was yet so much to do. She wished the police chief were here to help her make the right decisions. But he had insisted, "Our job is to keep an eye on the neighborhood. Your job will be to start the watch so the neighbors can help one another."

The grammar school about five blocks away had volunteered their grounds for the softball game. The stick ball and tug-of-war were to be held there later in the afternoon. Candy directed a group with softball hats, gloves, and bats in that direction. Someone passing by perched a green baseball hat on Candy's head.

Though it was only eleven-thirty, the streets were gradually filling, until Candy turned around and found small groups walking about in every direction. They were coming out of houses, sitting on stoops watching, standing on the corners talking to one another. Bicycles stood stacked next to motorcycles.

For the first time in a long time, Aunt Betty's neighbors came out of their homes to greet one another. Most of them were carrying plates, bags, old toys, plants, and boxes of soda.

A new aroma drifted up the streets, a surprise even to Candy. A hot-food truck with hamburgers and hot dogs, hot pretzels and cotton candy, parked on the corner and was immediately met by hungry customers. New tables were set up with additional surprises as one family after another added their contribution.

The food table held Chinese egg rolls, home-made Indian food, pasta, and stuffed cabbage. Candy herself ate an egg roll for nourishment, and had her face painted like a cat's.

Candy stood beind the table with all the fliers about the neighborhood watch piled in a box. There were buttons and badges and decals. An empty piece of paper with a pencil beside it encouraged everyone to sign up as volunteers. The sign propped up on the table stated, "Sign up here to assist the neighborhood watch. It's your program."

The paper looked almost empty, however, and Candy worried that it might stay that way. The block party was fun, but its initial purpose was to get the program started. They needed volunteers to do that. Hour by hour, she returned to the table, hoping signatures would fill the sheets of paper. Gradually, ever so slowly, a name was written across the page under Volunteers. South Eighteenth Street was beginning to fill. Then South Nineteenth Street. Block captain after block captain began to cover the pages. An assistant here and there. Some streets had three people willing to participate. There was even a volunteer to coordinate the mobile townwatch. Someone offered to be on a telephone committee. An editor had signed up to do a monthly newsletter. By early afternoon Candy knew they had succeeded.

She had lost sight of Flip. She wanted to share the good news with him but the crowds around the PA system now prevented her from even catching a glimpse of his curly hair. She felt almost as if she were a spectator at a fair.

Faces passed her with painted flowers on cheeks, animals on foreheads, smiles and stripes on ears and noses and any place available. The face-painting lady was really busy. Older people were strolling up the streets; it might have been the boardwalk instead of the center of town. They stopped, chatted, tasted, and then walked on.

The lady in charge of the elephant sale was making a deal for the sale of an old lamp. She bargained with the buyer as the price of the lamp slid down. Young people danced in front of Flip's microphone, his voice now and then sounding out above the music, calling out to newcomers to join the festivities. His voice was like a connection she could feel all the way up the block.

So many things were going on at once. The man with the peanut cannon was busy also. There was always a group of people around him, watching the peanuts perform, flying into the air while everyone around reached out to catch them.

Linda raced by several times with a new boy in tow. Her face had lost the painted smiles and her hair was wet.

"What have you been doing?" Candy called.

"Apple dunking."

She hadn't counted on that event. Well, as long as people had fun. Some neighbors were actually bringing their own entertainment. A girl sat under a poplar tree, playing the guitar. A small group of admirers sat around her. Others perched on their stoop steps, watching, eating, resting, before they joined the throng of people now in the center of the street. Beach chairs rested on the sidewalk.

Candy rechecked the list on her table. It was now practically filled. She folded it up, put the paper in her pocket, and left another plain sheet in its place. She didn't want to lose the valuable names, now that she finally had them.

Aunt Betty had taken over the white elephant sale. Some women were gathered around her, examining a strand of imitation pearls Candy recognized as part of Aunt Betty's odds and ends.

"My name's Mrs. Simpson," she heard one of the women say. "I live across the street from you."

Aunt Betty smiled warmly in return. "Then this strand of beads must be a gift from one neighbor to another." She deposited the strand in the surprised woman's hands.

By then there must have been over three hundred people milling about in the streets. Someone took over the microphone and announced the time of the softball game. Teenagers sat along the curbs slurping water ice. When three o'clock came, many left the tables to go over to the field.

Candy and Linda joined the softball game, while Flip stayed behind with those who preferred to remain at the party.

"Hasn't it been a great day?" Linda asked. Her arms were loaded with potato chips and pretzels. "We've got to do this again up in our own neighborhood. Maybe next spring. I think I'll get in touch with the police chief and see what I can arrange."

Candy was astonished. Linda was actually taking the initiative for a change. Well, good! She didn't think right now she had the stamina to go through all of it again herself. Anyway, the old Linda would only have followed Candy's lead. It was a wonder and a comfort to have this new Linda for support and, now and then, to do the leading.

The field was crowded. The teams were chosen, while families sat on the ground, on blankets, on jackets, on each other's laps, eating sandwiches, picnic dinners, drinking from thermoses as if the day were balmy, the month June instead of April.

A small trophy would be given to the winner. It was a surprise to Candy, who had not known of any arrangements for it. She picked it up to read the inscription. It was just an inexpensive silver-looking cup, of course, but the words brought tears to her eyes. It read, "The Sergeant Miller Neighborhood Watch Team Trophy."

"Linda and I wanted him to be part of it also," Flip told Candy.

The park soon filled with fans, yelling, screaming, jumping up and down. It was a game that held more than its share of errors, but no one seemed to notice or care. Candy's mother presented the trophy to the winning team. The competitions came to an end about five-thirty and the crowd broke up, most going back to their homes.

Linda and Candy returned to the block party. The music was blaring, but the streets were no longer crowded. The tables had been cleared off, most of everything either eaten, or sold, or given away.

Chalk designs covered everything. Dried eggs from the egg toss lay along the curbs, intermingled with peanut shells and popcorn. Paper cups and cigarette butts cluttered the streets and spilled on to the sidewalks.

"Well, I guess it's up to us." Candy shrugged, exhausted, not feeling too enthusiastic about the gigantic housecleaning job facing the three of them.

Aunt Betty walked by with Mrs. Simpson. "This

place is a mess," she said, straightening her blue hat, a new plant under one arm. She took the woman's arm walking next to her, as if they were old friends, and they continued up the block in deep conversation. "But I think it was a grand success," she called back over her shoulder, the blue eyes twinkling.

Candy grabbed a plastic bag. When she looked up, she was surprised to see neighbors coming out of their houses again, as if the block party had just begun. But this time they were carrying brooms, hoses, dustpans, mops, and garbage buckets.

"They've come to help clean up," she said to Flip, who was busy unraveling a hose from one of the houses.

Buckets and scrub brushes were put to work. One broom after another passed by as strong arms pushed and swept up and down the street.

The music played on while those involved in cleaning up chatted with one another, making the job a little more bearable. Candy folded up another list of neighborhood watch volunteers and put it in her pocket. There would be enough now to give to the police chief, enough to ensure the success of the program and the involvement of Aunt Betty's neighbors.

The hot-dog man remained and served free hot dogs to the twenty helpers who remained. It took a couple of hours, but gradually the street was cleared of trash, the streets and sidewalks scrubbed clean, and all looked as it had been before. The roadblocks were removed. The drawings had vanished. Only the neighborhood watch sign remained. And something more.

Neighbors stood along the sidewalks talking to one another . . . there were smiles and handshakes. Candy was certain that though everything had returned to normal, it would never be the same again. The change was in attitude, in friendliness, in a oneness that extended all over South Eighteenth and South Nineteenth streets. She was confident that now they knew one another, the neighbors would continue to watch over one another and to care about one another's safety.

Standing there, she had the same feeling of victory that had come over her at Stanley High the day the dress guide was approved. Again, there were people surrounding her who cared about one another, who were willing to become involved and join forces to change things and make them better. She felt good inside. She had helped make it happen at Stanley High and now the neighborhood watch here. But without the cooperation of her classmates and here Aunt Betty's neighbors, Candy realized, she could not have changed it alone.

Flip was sitting on the curb, the broom resting on his legs. Candy sat down beside him. He still had the clown face painted on, the eyes with wide lashes, the cheeks bright red, polka dots over the forehead.

Candy still wore her painted-on whiskers and cat eyes.

"Will there ever be a Candy without a mask?" he asked, leaning his head on her shoulder.

"I guess you'll have to stick around and find out," she answered boldly.

The cat and the clown embraced each other and then kissed, right there on the corner of South Nineteenth Street.

About the Author

HARRIET MAY SAVITZ lives with her husband, daughter and son near Philadelphia, Pennsylvania. She grew up and attended school in New Jersey. She is the author of three other novels, including *The Lionhearted, Wait Until Tomorrow,* and *Run, Don't Walk* which became an ABC-TV afterschool special, several short stories, and a nonfiction book on wheelchair athletes. She is presently a member of the National Wheelchair Athletic Association and the Pennsylvania Wheelchair Athletic Association. Her ten-year experience working with the disabled and with wheelchair sports teams has enabled her to write sensitively about the problems and frustrations encountered by the handicapped as they enter the mainstream of life.